BECKET BRAMBLE AND THE PRINCES IN THE TOWER

Stephen Begg

ISBN: 1527206238
ISBN 13: 9781527206236

With thanks,
To all who helped:

Nadia Boucher, Mandy McAleese, Ben Paynter, Martyn Beardsley, Gavin Webb, TLC, Dave Perry, Hilary Johnson and of course my darling wife Lydia for all her patience.

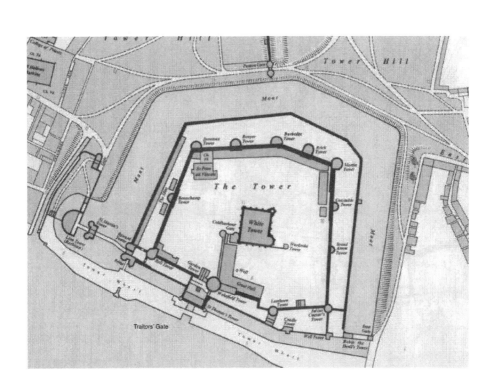

Traitors' Gate

ENGLAND 1483

Edward fidgeted at the table in the grubby inn in Stony Stratford, a stopover on the road to London. He was twelve years old and about to be King of England. Toying with his food impatiently, he thought of his mother; she would be waiting for him. It had been such a long time since he had seen her. He had been so young when he was sent away to live with his mother's brother, Lord Rivers, in his impressive castle in the West Country. Pushing away his plate, he ran his fingers through his hair - he couldn't believe he was to be king; it didn't seem real.

His uncle, Earl Rivers, was making the short journey to Northampton to meet up with his other uncle, Richard, his father's trusted lieutenant, who was joining them on the journey. He loved Rivers – he had been like a father to him. Edward knew he could trust him with his life and he was sure that he would safely deliver him to London ahead of his coronation. But what was keeping him so long?

Edward could barely remember Uncle Richard. He'd always lived in the north and had rarely come to court in London. But his father had loved his little brother and trusted him more than any man in the kingdom.

Edward pushed back his chair and trudged out into the cold morning air. Squinting into the glare of the low sun, he heard a faint rumble and out of the morning mist came two riders, their immense warhorses splashing through the mud, their nostrils breathing a fiery mist.

As they approached, Edward noticed that they were followed by a troop of soldiers on horseback. He strained his eyes and pulled his cloak tightly around him as the men came into view. Who were they? Where was Rivers? Something wasn't right and suddenly the men were upon him. Two servants came running and grabbed at the reins, grappling with the giant, rearing horses as the riders hastily dismounted.

A small, athletic man approached him.

"Good morning, Your Highness. I trust I find you well. Unfortunately we need to show great haste. London is many hours ride away."

"Good morning, uncle. Pray, where is Rivers?"

"He has been detained at Northampton along with the other conspirators."

"Conspirators? You cannot mean Rivers. What conspiracy?"

Richard clenched his gloved fists. "We have to hurry. We need to get you to London before your mother and her family stir up any more rebellion."

"My mother? Rebellion?" Edward was scared.

"I will explain once we are on the road," his uncle stated tersely.

Edward was helped into the saddle of his chestnut pony and they set off down the muddy road to London.

The pony battled gamely through the puddles, splattering Edward's face and clothes as he looked back for Rivers. There was no sign. The only people he had faith in were left behind in Northampton.

It didn't make sense. His father had always loved Richard - he must have his best interests at heart? The world suddenly felt a dangerous place. Why had his father died? If he were still alive he wouldn't be in this mess. And why had mother fled and sought the protection of the church?

The second man introduced himself as Henry Stafford, Duke of Buckingham. He seemed very pleased with himself, laughing and making jokes, but Edward wasn't listening – his protected world had collapsed around him. The sun finally began to rise and Edward wiped his nose with his glove, staring fixedly ahead, his heart thumping as the hooves of his pony trumped through the sodden English countryside.

CHAPTER 1

THE TRAIN TO YORK

Becket woke up with a jolt – his head banging on the train window. He was wide- awake in a moment- it was always this way. His mouth was dry and beside him lay the remains of the dry and curly egg sandwich the welfare officer had provided.

"The next stop will be Doncaster," announced a guard over the speaker system.

One more stop and they would be in York. Becket had been asleep almost the whole journey. The train glided past grey, bland houses, their gardens full of hanging washing. Becket re-read the crumpled letter his aunt had sent him.

It had been a year ago that they had first met at the funeral of his parents. Mad Aunt Lizzie was his dad's elder sister. Becket was not sure she was actually mad, but she had seemed a bit witch-like - not with the regular black cape, broomstick and pointed hat, but in the strange manner she had spoken. Her voice, no more than a whisper - her vacant stare as if in some sort of trance.

Becket's head felt heavy as he remembered the funeral. His parents had both been teachers: his dad a history lecturer at the local university and his mum, a PE teacher at Becket's own, run-down comprehensive school. Dad was mad on history and Mum was mad on Dad.

Time hadn't healed the hurt. He was twelve years old and being an only child was quite alone. Aunt Lizzie had come to the funeral and stood beside the vicar as the coffins were lowered into the ground - the three of them silent. Becket hadn't cried. He hadn't known what to feel. He was lost. His aunt had led him slowly through the dew-moistened grass of the graveyard to the waiting taxi in silence. What followed was a blur of piteous stares and comforting words. It had been a long year.

The carriage was empty apart from an old lady crammed into the seat across the aisle. She was immersed in bags and was wearing a green tea cosy hat, brown wellies and, despite it being early summer, a heavy coat that would have kept her warm in the depths of winter at the North Pole. Consequently, she had very red rosy cheeks and seemed to be short of breath; and by the sound of the gasping noises emanating from beneath her thick scarf, it would be touch and go if she survived the journey. She smiled at Becket.

Becket looked down at his battered suitcase covered in NBA basketball stickers. He was leaving little behind. The stark room that he shared at the school boarding house had never felt real – almost as if he were acting out a sad film and the credits would return him to normal. He had missed the small, red- brick, mid-terraced house where he had lived all his life – it had been his home. It was sold with all its contents to pay the crippling mortgage. His dad had never been good with money and had spent all he earned on his passion - visiting medieval ruins, battlefields and castles. He was always starting to write a new book – 'this was the one that was going to change our lives forever.'

Becket's life had changed forever and now all he had in the world was in the battered suitcase at his feet and his peculiar Aunt Lizzie.

To help deaden the annoying chatter of a portly bald man in an ill-fitting suit who had got on at Doncaster, Becket looked inside the brown leather case. Apart from his clothes was a book called *The Concise Guide to The Kings and Queens of England,* a photograph of his parents, taken that last Christmas at the Tower of London where they had tried unsuccessfully to teach him to ice skate, some old NBA basketball magazines, a small satchel filled with all sorts of odds and ends and his beloved trainers. His mum had bought them for Becket as a reward for winning the district cross-country trial, a race he had won by a full five minutes despite competing against some older boys. This had made his mum extremely proud and his dad compare him to some Ancient Greek athlete nobody had ever heard of. Becket cared for his trainers above all else; they were black and red and very cool.

Becket had rarely looked through the tatty satchel, but as the train sped northwards he decided it was better than listening to the droning man or wondering how long it would take the old lady to explode or burst into flames from the heat of the carriage.

Inside was a pencil case containing some foreign coins and a Swiss Army penknife. There were also a few puncture repair kits, lots of old lollipop sticks, a dozen bottles of bubble-making liquid, some rather mouldy whizz bangs and several packets of balloons. Hardly a treasure trove and in truth Becket was a little ashamed of his childish keepsakes, but he never liked to throw anything away.

Becket opened the book about the Kings and Queens of England, given to him by his father, and read the scribbled inscription inside:

'To the Sainted Becket, the boy who has been here before.' Love Mum and Dad, July 25th 2015.

It had been a tenth birthday present. He slammed the book shut. A tear pricked his eye. Why had his parents gone on that last trip?

Becket's parents had decided to have a second honeymoon, retracing the steps of King Richard the Lion Heart's crusade to the Holy Land. They had departed during the first week of last year's summer holidays, condemning him to the drudge of summer school, and within a few days, disaster had struck. Their tour bus crashed into a ditch on its way to Jerusalem, killing everyone on board.

He thought back to the day of the funeral. Aunt Lizzie had sat him down in the scruffy front room of the little terraced house and explained to him,

"Becket, I can't take you back to York with me just yet." She looked awkward. "I'm sorry. I hope you understand?"

He couldn't look at her. His belly was a mess of swirls, mirroring the pattern on the brown-orange embossed 1970s wallpaper. He wanted to cry.

"Trust me, I will send for you as soon as I can. My house in York is now your home too, but you have to give me time. I have a few difficult issues I have to … find a way to deal with, but I promise you won't be left alone for long."

Becket's aunt had pushed a small box toward him. He looked up at her almost frightened eyes.

Becket removed the pale tissue paper carefully and out plopped a heavy pendant on a frayed leather chain. It fitted into the palm of his hand, and had a large ruby-like stone about five centimetres wide set in the centre of a gold Star of David design. Dotted around its edge were eight much smaller stones of a paler purple colour and to its centre was the odd jagged outline where a jewel had been gouged out.

"Keep it safe, Becket. A token of trust … until I send for you. Please be patient."

It had been a year. An awful year. A year of jibes and fights. Of bullying and empty promises. Becket twiddled his long almost-white tousled locks around his finger. It had become a habit. It hadn't been cut since they had died. His brown eyes moistened, there were like his mother's, lightening in the centre, like a half-eaten Christmas caramel. The serious, haunted expression on a thin, pale face, was his dad's along with the long pointed nose. His classmates poked fun at him, calling him "Big Nose Bramble." His dad had said, he should be proud of his Roman nose, that he should never be ashamed of his ancestry. But he wasn't the one being called "Concorde nose".

Becket had often been bullied at school even before his parents' death. Being the son of a teacher wasn't much fun.

"Mummy's boy!" they would shout at him and "Teacher's pet!" His mum had worked him extra hard during PE and that meant he was very fit, easily winning the long cross-country races she was so fond of making his class endure. She didn't help his popularity - his classmates called him a freak and the names and taunts just got worse.

The kids at school had left him alone after the funeral. They didn't know what to say. When he entered the room and they would look away. He had no close friends, but that suited him. Becket had always been happy in his own company and being a rather sensible sort of boy, his father had often said, "Becket, you've been here before!"

The train rumbled on. York – a place he'd only been to once before on a rainy holiday with his parents, dragged along in the ageing Ford Mondeo. The memories were not fond ones - there had been an awful lot of charging around the countryside in damp waterproofs and trudging through fields in search of an ancient stone or the remains of a castle wall. Being an only child wasn't much fun. He looked at the passing houses and wondered what Aunt Lizzie's place would be like. He was glad she had finally sent for him.

A week ago he had been called into the Headmaster's office. Mr Franks had stared at Becket over his glasses, analysing him for any show of emotion. He passed Becket a small envelope. Inside was a smudged letter. It stated simply that Becket was to come to York in one week, followed by some directions and an address, signed by his aunt. No friendly greeting of reassurance. Just the stark details and a train ticket.

The guard announced that the train was approaching York. Becket twisted his pendant in his hands, feeling the smoothness of the central stone, it seemed to calm him. He had been too embarrassed to wear the feminine trinket but had kept it in his pocket and close to him. Maybe it was a good luck charm from centuries ago and had mystical powers that would protect him always.

Becket scolded himself for being such a dreamer as the train ground to a shuddering halt in York. He gathered his small collection of belongings, shut his suitcase and looked with distaste at the remains of the evil-looking egg sandwich, worrying whether the Accident and Emergency department at York Hospital would be crowded at this time of day.

The bald, sweaty man in his now crumpled suit dashed past Becket and the doddery old lady, almost knocking her to the floor. Becket gallantly helped her down the step and she gave him a warm smile and thanked him.

Becket jumped down onto the crowded platform and rifled through his pockets in search of the letter his aunt had sent him, then headed for the bus that would take him to her house and his new life.

CHAPTER 2
THE OLD GATEHOUSE

The bus pulled away from York station. Aunt Lizzie lived a few miles to the south of the city centre, so the journey would not be a long one. Becket twiddled his hair pondering what lay in store. *The Old Gatehouse, Swinford Wood,* didn't sound particularly appealing nor did a life with an ageing aunt, but he immersed himself in a well-thumbed basketball magazine, ignoring the disappearing squat terraced houses and the never-ending pale green fields that had begun to surround the bus.

He had read the magazine hundreds of times, but he loved basketball. Although short of stature, Becket's constant practice in the gym after school and the fact that the games master had a crush on his mum earned him a place in the school team. Unfortunately, they weren't very good and defeat followed defeat, but it didn't quash his love for the game.

Twenty minutes into the journey, the bus halted at yet another stop. It seemed to have stopped a hundred times.

"This is your stop lad," shouted the driver.

Becket looked out of the windows at the open fields and dense woodland on either side.

"Are you sure?"

"Yep, this is the stop for Swinford Manor. The main gate is down that road yonder, but you'll find the old gatehouse through that footpath in the wood," he said, pointing at a rather narrow path to the right hand side of the bus.

Picking up his suitcase, Becket stepped off the bus and watched it disappear into the distance. He was in the middle of nowhere. This couldn't be right. The footpath was overgrown and didn't look very inviting. Aunt Lizzie had seemed a bit eccentric, but who would want to live here?

The footpath soon widened into a gravel track that was slowly being reclaimed by plants and weeds. It must have been the original driveway to the manor house, as looking up, Becket saw in front of him, two oak trees framing some tall, rusted iron gates. To the side of these gates, sitting back almost hiding in the wood, was a small house. It had to be Aunt Lizzie's place - the Old Gatehouse.

Becket's new home was as odd as its location. It looked like three tiny houses stuck together at right angles and had three pointed façades that were topped with a startling weathered stone boar's head. It gave him the creeps. A series of narrow windows were forced into the crumbling red and yellow brickwork, and dressing all the windows were the thickest of net curtains, making it impossible to see inside.

Becket forced himself to the sturdy oak front door. The large, rusted knocker, yet another boar's head, glared down at him. He knocked and waited. No reply. He tried again. Nothing. Twisting the iron handle, Becket shouldered open the heavy door. Inside, he was hit by a welcoming whiff of lavender and apart from the soft ticking of a mantel clock, all was quiet. Becket looked around the room. Directly in front of him, sitting on the dark wooden floorboards, were an old golden coloured patterned sofa, a mahogany coffee table and a couple of small, circular, threadbare discoloured rugs. The house felt damp and cold. Opposite the front door was a narrow staircase leading to the bedrooms above. Becket walked into the kitchen. From the beamed ceiling hung bunches of herbs, and a stack of coloured jars full of peculiar plants and liquids were jammed on shelves beside an old butler-style sink. Thankfully there was no broomstick and no sign of a black cat, but Becket had never seen such an unusual house. Where was his aunt? Maybe he had got the wrong day? Then he spied a note scribbled in red ink lying on an oak table.

> *Dear Becket*
>
> *I have been called away to a meeting. I am so sorry that I'm not here to greet you. It is quite likely I will be back very late. Please help yourself to anything you would like from the fridge.*
>
> *You will find your bedroom on the right at the top of the stairs. If suits, take a look around Swinford Wood. It is not very large, so you won't get lost.*
>
> *But be sure to avoid the manor house as Mr Parker, the steward is a bit of a busybody and does not tolerate trespassing.*
>
> *Don't wait up. I will see you at breakfast.*
> *Aunt Elizabeth.*

Becket checked the fridge, but he wasn't hungry. His belly was making the weirdest of noises was, probably the revenge of the evil egg sandwich.

He decided to explore the rest of the house. At the far end of the sitting room, next to the staircase, was an "L" shaped hallway leading to a heavy door. The hallway was freezing, much colder than the rest of the house. He pulled at the door, but it was locked. There was no key. Shivering, he went back to the sitting room. It was too early for bed so he decided to investigate the wood. It had already been a long day and he felt a little crabby as he strolled aimlessly in and out of the trees kicking at the fallen leaves. His thoughts drifted to his parents; his dad, head as usual in a book, hair sticking up, clicking his teeth as he often did when he was concentrating and his mum's latest disastrous concoction, courtesy of the latest cookery programme. He fondly recalled a runny lasagne and the charred, inedible onion and marmite stuffing she had so proudly presented last Christmas.

A high-pitched screeching noise interrupted his thoughts. Was it a bird? But it was very loud - like an animal in pain, crying out for help. It was getting shriller and more frantic. Perhaps he could help. Becket walked toward the noise, but found a high, redbrick wall topped with jagged broken glass blocking his path. It had to be the surrounding wall to Swinford Manor. His aunt had warned him about trespassing, but Becket had to try and help. He looked up, but it was far too high to climb and the sharp glass at the top would cut his hands to ribbons. To his left, was a good climbing tree and Becket easily clambered to the top. He could see for miles. Below him sat a sprawling, rectangular manor house built of red brick and covered with thick ivy. It's chunky chimneys and assortment of shaped windows making it look more like an oversized old steam ship than a house. The formal lawns and hedges were well kept, but there were no flowers in the beds and no sign of life anywhere. Becket quivered. It was almost as if he were looking at a postcard. The whole scene seemed without substance, almost like a theatre curtain – a distraction waiting to be drawn. He saw a flicker at one of the wide leaded windows. He squinted, but the grey glass just stared blankly back. Maybe a trick of the light, but it looked like a figure, hooded and stooped. A silhouette of an old lady in a dark hooded gown, faceless, staring out of the window and straight at him. An icy flutter rose in Becket's chest making him almost lose his balance. He grabbed the branch tightly.

Then, he heard voices arguing below. Two men, close to the boundary wall. The shorter one seemed annoyed and was reprimanding a taller, thinner man as a dog came sniffing out of the bushes. Becket kept as still as the bowing branch would allow. He wanted to climb down, to get back to his aunt's, but his legs wouldn't budge. This had been a stupid idea. The shorter man stopped to take a call on his mobile phone and walked back toward the house. Becket looked back to the window. The curtains had been pulled. The screeching noise had stopped.

Becket was spooked, losing his balance, he fell from the branch and grazed his shins on the trunk as he slid to the ground. Inspecting his cuts, he looked around and realised that he had absolutely no idea which way was home. All the trees looked the same. What was he going to do?

The cloud-barred sky was now fading to a sombre grey and the wind held a new chill. The wood suddenly seemed less hospitable, as if it was closing in on him. He started to run, crunching through the leaves, stumbling on broken branches, pushing his way through the undergrowth until he tripped and fell headlong into a bush. He had to get a grip. This was ridiculous. Then he saw a black spider scurrying for the safety of his hoodie. Becket leapt up, brushing himself down and shaking like a demented dancer.

He was terrified of spiders. He hated them, and sometimes woke up in the middle of the night, screaming and flapping at imaginary creepy-crawlies. Shuddering, he straightened his clothes and walked back to the wall of the manor. If he kept close to the wall he was bound to come to his aunt's house. And sure enough, nestled in the trees in front of him, there it was. Becket almost fell through the front door. His knees throbbed and his head banged. There was still no sign of his aunt so after a much needed glass of water, he went straight up to his bedroom. It had been a long day. Collapsing onto the single bed, he pushed his face deep into the pillow and was snoring in seconds.

CHAPTER 3
AUNT LIZZIE

B ecket awoke with the sun shining on his face. For a moment he was unsure where he was. It was so quiet. Still fully dressed, he went downstairs. There was no sign of his aunt, and the only sound was the tick-tocking of the mantel clock. It was six o' clock. She was probably still asleep. Becket went into the kitchen and poured himself a glass of juice.

He drifted into the sitting room and sat down on the thread-bare sofa. What was he going to do today? Yesterday hadn't been much fun, with the dull train journey, getting lost in the wood and the freaky manor house. Had he really seen a figure at the window? His aunt would know who lived there. He snaked around the sitting room looking at the old ornaments and photographs until he remembered the room at the back of the house.

He went into the small L-shaped hall and this time found a key in the lock. The heavy door opened without a sound. Just like the rest of the house, the room was dimly lit, and as his eyes narrowed, he was startled to see, across the room what appeared to be a bulky figure staring back at him. The form stood motionless and silent. It looked like an alien, with a large swollen head, bulky body, thin legs and over-sized feet. Becket took a deep breath and stepped further into the room. The apparition held its ground and made no attempt to move. Becket edged further in, straining his eyes. It couldn't be his aunt – could it? Looking closer, he rubbed his clammy hands on his jeans and switched on a nearby lamp. What an idiot! It was just a suit of armour mounted on a plinth. The scare at the manor house was playing on his mind. He pulled back the heavy curtains from the window, but they only revealed a boarded window. Switching on the main light, Becket laughed at his own stupidity.

The place was a treasure trove of ancient artefacts. The shelves were crammed with dusty books, rows of silver goblets, copper bowls and different shaped pots. He had never seen such things before other than in display cases in stately homes and castles. On a large wooden table in the middle of the room lay a pile of faded maps, a heavy red leather-bound book, and in one corner sat a mannequin wearing a long flowing dress of purple satin. On a leather armchair was a cushion embroidered with small gold birds, and sitting on a side table there was a copper bowl full of different shaped coins. Becket couldn't resist grabbing a handful, allowing them to slip through his fingers and jangle back into the bowl. Where did his aunt get all this stuff? Underneath the chair lay an assortment of shabby leather shoes and boots, and to its left, propped in the corner, was a huge sword, a battle-axe and a wooden crossbow riddled with woodworm. What fun it would be to take them into the forest and pretend to be a knight in shining armour. Perhaps his aunt had been collecting these things for decades? He took down a book and blowing away the dust, opened it. The intricate writing was impossible to understand. Taking down another, he found it was a small prayer book, with illustrated margins. All of these pieces must be centuries old. It explained why his aunt had kept the room locked. He opened the big book on the table and although the greasy cover and yellowing paper seemed equally aged, some of the writing inside seemed more recent. Becket toyed with his pendant as he leaned over the book trying to decipher the scribble. His aunt's gift didn't seem so odd now that he had seen the room; she must have spent a lifetime visiting antiques fairs and boot sales collecting all these things. He started to read, but his eyes began to water, blurring the page. It was so cold. He rubbed his running nose and blinked. The room felt smaller, airless, like it was crowding in on him and his eyes were struggling to focus. He suddenly had to get out. Lurching from the room, he headed back to the warmth of the sitting room, throwing himself down onto the sofa. He clasped his head in his hands, but the room wouldn't stop spinning. Then, he heard a voice from the stairway.

"Good morning, Becket," said Aunt Lizzie, looking down at him with an enquiring smile. "Are you feeling quite well?"

Becket looked up at his aunt. She looked a little bedraggled, her long wispy grey hair with its bizarre fringe consisting of two sizeable curls: one dark red, and the other a startling dove-white hung loosely over her face - the same dark brown, almost black eyes as his dad peeping out. She wore a creased black dress with a jade-green shawl around her shoulders and her fingers were smothered in colourful rings.

"You look awfully pale," she continued as she descended the stairs, pushing her hair out of her eyes and joining him on the sofa.

"I felt dizzy and cold all of a sudden," answered Becket, hugging himself and beginning to feel a little better.

His aunt's smile disappeared.

"I see that you are wearing the pendant I gave you. I am so sorry it has taken me so long to send for you, but I had some business to deal with that took much longer than I had hoped."

"Have you eaten?" she asked.

Becket's confessed that he hadn't eaten anything since the train journey.

"You must eat, Becket! No wonder you feel so giddy. Come and sit in the kitchen and I will make you some breakfast. It would appear that we are the last of the Brambles and we ought to find out a little bit more about each other."

Aunt Lizzie sat down next to him and explained that she had lived in the house for over ten years. She had previously lived in a bungalow near his new school, but the noise of the children had been a constant source of annoyance. One day the children had started chanting that she was a witch, so enough was enough and it was time to move. She he had found this odd little house quite by chance and immediately fell in love with the seclusion of the surrounding wood and with York just a short bus ride away, all her needs were catered for.

"It was very sad about Alfred and your mother," sighed his aunt. "You must feel lost and alone. I will do all I can to make you feel that you have a home and a family. You will forgive some of my ways - I have been living alone for such a long, long time."

Becket's aunt asked him if he had managed to find his way around the house and if he needed anything. Becket warmed to her immediately. She looked a bit weird, but she had kind eyes.

"Aunt," asked Becket, "the room at the back of the house - the one that's full of all the ancient books and things - is that a museum?"

Her face clouded. "How did you get into that room?"

"There was a key in the door and ..."

She frowned angrily, but checking herself, she whispered,

"Oh! I must have left the key in the lock last night. The contents of that room are very precious to me. Please don't go in there again without my permission. I have had a lot problems with people trying to break in ..."

Becket thought of the boarded window. Who would want to break into this funny little house? Aunt Lizzie fell silent and came

15

closer. He could smell the faint scent of soap as she inspected his pendant closely, turning it over and over with her long, thin fingers.

"That room is part of my life Becket. There are pieces from all through the centuries. Like the pendant you are wearing, each piece has its own story to tell. When your father and I were little we both became fascinated by history. Your father always had his nose in his books and would roam around the fields where we grew up looking at old ruins. That's where we differed so much. I always felt and still feel that you should live history. These things were worn and used by real people and they all have a story to tell us."

His aunt seemed excited as she explained further, "You need to remember, however grand, however humble, history is being written every day by all sorts of people. It's hard to go forward in life without learning the lessons of the past."

His aunt reminded him a lot of his dad. Becket really missed his parents.

"Did you investigate the wonders of our wood?" asked his aunt.

Becket thought about being in the tree and the spectre at the window.

"Who lives at the manor house? It seems totally deserted."

Aunt Lizzie started. "Becket, the manor is not a place for children."

"But…but I just wondered…"

"No good will come of you going to that place. Please stay away from there."

She agitatedly pulled her shawl tightly around her shoulders and smoothed her unkempt fringe into order.

Becket thought she seemed almost fearful of the manor. It didn't make any sense.

"I have a nice surprise for you, Becket. I have bought you a present."

His aunt led him out of the front door to the rear of the house. She pulled off an old tarpaulin to reveal a remarkable looking bike.

"I'm afraid it's only second-hand, but the buses here aren't very regular, so I thought it would be a good and fun way for you to get around."

What a great bike! Becket loved its retro high-rise handlebars, its long padded high-back seat and three-speed gear lever that was coolly mounted on the crossbar. It had chunky mudguards and wide tyres, the front of which was smaller than the back. It looked like a Harley-Davidson motorbike and Becket fondly remembered placing ice-lolly sticks in the spokes of his old bike to create a noise like a motorbike engine. He would race along the lane at the back of his street pretending to be in a speedway race, much to the annoyance of the local dogs and their owners who used the alley as a pooch lavatory.

"It's called a Chopper. They were all the rage back in the 1970's. It's in such good condition that I thought it might do," explained his aunt.

Becket climbed aboard.

"Can I try it out?" he asked.

His aunt laughed, "Of course, but bring yourself back for lunch around one o'clock."

He spent the remainder of the morning racing through the wood. The Chopper handled the rough paths easily apart from an awful screech every time he slammed on the brakes. He pretended he was a knight on his trusty steed, rushing into battle, and stopped to pick up a broken branch that made a makeshift jousting pole. He charged at imaginary evil black knights, which in reality were just low-hanging branches and the odd lazy pigeon.

After a happy few hours, Becket returned home for lunch to find his aunt in the kitchen. He could smell the most appalling stink wafting through the house. It reminded him of school dinners and the hateful over-cooked broccoli.

His aunt was vigorously stirring all manner of steaming pots and pans, each of them throwing out a horrendous pong.

Aunt Lizzie was humming tunelessly to herself. "Lunch is almost ready," she said.

Becket eyed the evil-smelling pots.

"Oh don't worry, that's not lunch! They are my special herbal remedies," laughed his aunt. "There's plenty of bread and ham on the table."

"Herbal remedies?" asked Becket.

"Medicine made from herbs. All the ingredients in these pots I gathered from the wood. The recipes have been handed down through the ages."

Becket thought of the books he had come across in the secret room.

"In this pot is nettle tea. It has great health producing qualities and is almost as good as my cider vinegar," said his aunt stirring a green liquid. "I have a mixture of wormwood and mint which is wonderful for tummy pains. I'm making elderberry cordial, which helps keep all your sniffles at bay and is much better for you than all the expensive packets you will find in the chemist's."

He looked at a pile of dandelions.

"Dandelions are a great help for my arthritis. It's not much fun getting old, Becket."

Next to the sink, he noticed a bowl of the most bizarre-looking plants. They were circular, white and covered in thorns, each with a shocking sprout of purple spiky leaves poking out of their top.

His aunt followed his gaze. "That's burdock. If you eat something poisonous, it will come to the rescue - as will mulberry leaves mixed with vinegar."

"I thought you might ride into York this afternoon Becket?" said his aunt, as she tidied away the dishes. "It's only about a thirty minute cycle ride and a very easy journey."

Becket wondered what he would do in York, but was glad of the chance to ride on his new bike. His dad had told him that York had once been one of the mightiest medieval cities in Britain and had once been the capital of the north.

"You must feel very lost without your mum and dad, Becket," said his aunt. "I've always found when I felt I was losing my way in life or needed time to think clearly, that the Minster in York was the perfect place to visit. It can be inspiring and magical."

Becket was sure his dad had mentioned York Minster, but he was sure he had never visited it.

"The Minster," started his aunt, "is the largest cathedral in Northern Europe. There has been a place of worship there since Roman times."

Becket groaned. He feared he was in for a long lecture and eyed the bike through the window.

"The Gothic structure that stands today dates back to the thirteenth century." His aunt was clearly an expert on the Minster. "It contains some of the finest large stained-glass windows in the world."

He had seen way too many stained-glass windows.

"The exercise will do you good," she added. 'But be careful and make sure you're back before dark."

Yet another church, but at least he could escape the stench of his aunt's kitchen and the latent threat of being turned into a croaking frog.

"I have drawn you a map," said his aunt, passing him a scrap of paper. "It's very easy to find. Just take the road out of the wood and you will soon see a shop, which is Swinford Stores. Ask for the York road - you can't lose your way."

Becket took the map.

"You will find my purse on the table there. I have not much need of money," explained his aunt tasting a spoonful of steaming green gloop from the saucepan.

"But I expect you will need to buy a snack from the store, so take what you need. I found this old guidebook of York which you may find useful; and if you wouldn't mind picking up a packet of caustic soda for me from the store as I find it's the only thing that gets this sink of mine really sparkling."

Becket took some coins from his aunt's purse.

"Oh and please ask old Mrs Askey if my order of apple cider vinegar has arrived," she shouted after him, as he jumped on his bike and pedalled away down the gravel drive.

After about a mile, he saw the shop his aunt had mentioned. The eyes of the old lady at the counter, lit up behind her thick, dark-rimmed glasses, surprised at the appearance of her young customer. The shop was crammed full of useful things and by the look of some of the dust on the tins and bottles, quite a lot of things people had never needed. Becket was soon filling his satchel with the simple provisions the shop could provide, which included some chocolate and a can of fizzy drink (luxuries his parents rarely allowed), not forgetting his aunt's caustic soda.

"Anything else?" the old lady asked him, licking the ends of her stubby fingers.

Becket saw a small torch and thought maybe it would come in useful. Mrs Askey seemed pleased with her sales and caressed the money into the till as he threw his satchel around his neck. She pointed out the York road and Becket raced off.

The wind grew stronger and turned to rain. Becket was soon soaked.

He gritted his teeth and put his head down to the wind. It couldn't be much further.

Then from behind him, Becket heard a car or a van. He slowed down, catching his breath, and waited for it to pass; but the driver appeared to be content to crawl along behind him. Maybe he should stop and let the vehicle pass? It came closer and closer and suddenly accelerated past with a roar – but far too close! The wing-mirror hit Becket's handlebars, sending him crashing off the road and into a pool of muddy water at the bottom of a ditch.

He picked himself up slowly, feeling a shooting pain in his right knee. The bike wasn't damaged, and as he righted it on the road he noticed a white van had stopped ahead of him. It began to reverse. The driver must be coming back to see if he was OK. The window rolled down and a spotty face with a toothy grin shouted, "That's what nosey boys who climb trees get for their trouble! There'll be more to come if you don't mind your own business."

Becket couldn't believe it. This man had deliberately forced him off the road. Before he could react the van sped off with another clanking of gears.

Becket was shaken. That must have been one of the men from the manor. They'd seen him in the tree after all. His aunt had been right to warn him.

Becket was tempted to turn back for home. He was soaked and now his knee was throbbing, but decided to continue his journey. "Bullies never prosper!" he could hear his mum's voice echoing in his mind.

The fields soon became shops and houses and the traffic grew busier. Grumbling buses passed close by and Becket saw a tall stone tower with an arched gate in the middle of the road. It looked like a mini castle, with two impressive turrets standing ten metres above the road. A sign said Micklegate, one of the ancient entrances to the town of York. His dad had told him that a stone wall surrounded the medieval city and there were several similar gates dotted around the perimeter. The tower had cross-shaped narrow windows and Becket imagined ancient archers standing ready with their longbows. His dad had delighted in scaring him with the gruesome tales of traitors' severed heads being placed on spikes on top of the gates as a warning to others. He shivered in the drizzle and thought of how awful it would have been to witness such a horrific sight.

He cycled through the arched gateway, over a bridge and crossed the River Ouse. A motorised train packed with tourists went past him on the road. The tour guide, wearing a cowboy hat to protect himself from the rain, was giving a lecture on York, and yet more tourists were wandering along the city wall. Passing through yet another gate, he cycled down a narrow cobbled street that opened into a wide square, where he stopped and looked up at the most extraordinary cathedral. It was enormous, dwarfing the surrounding houses and hotels. He had arrived at York Minster.

CHAPTER 4
THE MINSTER

Becket was awestruck. He had often visited St Paul's Cathedral in London with his parents, but the size and splendour of the building standing in front of him was astonishing. The rain teemed down on the Minster's pale yellowing stone as he gawped at the two sixty metre Gothic towers that framed the front entrance. Behind them was an equally tall rectangular tower that seemed to be missing its own Gothic spire, as if a giant had lopped it off like the top of a huge boiled egg. Jumping off his bike next to a busy, square green, he parked the Chopper next to a row of bikes chained to the railings. There was no padlock, but he was reassured by an old lady, oddly indifferent to the rain, sitting on a nearby bench. She was munching her way through a brown paper bag seemingly full of cakes, pork pies and goodness knows what else. She attempted to say something, but only managed to splutter a mouthful of crumbs onto the floor, providing a welcome feast for the grateful waiting pigeons. She then succumbed to a coughing fit and Becket had to resist the urge to give her a slap on the back.

"Don't worry young man, your bike will be safe here. I will keep an eye on it for you," she offered through a mouthful of sticky chocolate brownie.

There was a long queue of tourists at the main entrance to the Minster. Becket hoped that the line would move quickly. He was drenched and cold. Looking up at the towers looming above him, he saw a number of gargoyles, perched on its worn bricks. They seemed ready to swoop down on the unwary tourists at any minute like mini stone dragons.

The line moved swiftly and he was soon inside, but to his annoyance, Becket noticed a kiosk selling tickets. He only had a few coins left. How stupid he had been! Not relishing the thought of going back out into the rain, he was just wondering what he should do next when a grey haired man behind the roped barrier asked in a gravelly voice, "Becket?"

"Err... yes."

"I've been expecting you," he answered, smiling jovially.

Becket wondered who this oddball was. His head a mass of grey curls partially hidden by a smart bowler hat, his bushy moustache and sideburns, framing a wrinkled and careworn face. He was wearing a very formal starched black jacket, with a high-buttoned waistcoat and a velvet bow tie.

The man pulled the rope barrier aside to allow him through.

Becket hesitated, "Shouldn't I buy a ticket?"

"Don't worry about such things, my lad. As I said, I have been expecting you."

Maybe he was a friend of his aunt's - one of the swarms of guides that were rushing up and down the aisles? Either way, Becket was pleased to be able to dry out.

"Let me give you a little tour of this wondrous place young fellow," volunteered the old man. "It won't be as dull as you imagine."

Why was he always being dragged around churches and why was everybody he met so obsessed with boring him with history?

He was led down the aisle, the old man pointing up at the stained-glass windows with his stick, explaining their origins.

Becket wasn't really listening, but thought the vivid colours were striking.

"Now this," gushed the old man, "is the absolute highlight of the Minster for me."

He pointed up to a long stone row of figures perched on a ledge about ten feet above the ground. They all wore gold crowns with unruly hair sticking out beneath.

"This, my boy, is the Quire Screen. As you can see, there are fifteen statues in total and they stand in chronological order, each one being a former king of England. Furthest on the left is William the Conqueror, 1066 and all that, and to the far right, the last statue is Henry VI, a very pious king, who became embroiled in the Wars of the Roses. York and Lancaster and all that good stuff."

Becket looked at the figures uneasily. They were grotesque. The dull colourless eyes made them look like zombies from a late night horror film.

An archway split the medieval screen: eight statues to the left side and seven to the right, and above the screen sat an organ, which began to boom out. It added to the creepiness of the place. Becket was glad to move away from the noise when the old man asked him if he would like to climb the tower.

"There are 275 steps, but you look like a fit young fellow."

There was a long queue of tourists and sign saying *NEXT TOUR 3pm.*

The old man ignored both and led him up the steps of the tower. He seemed to almost glide up with little need of his walking stick - that was, until part of the way up, he suddenly turned to face Becket, brandishing the stick and swishing it like a sword.

"*En garde!*" he boomed.

Becket took a step back in surprise.

"Becket, you see how the stairs ascend in a clockwise direction? That's so the soldiers defending the tower have more space to wield their swords in their *right* hands. The attackers chasing them would have very little room to fight back, as the centre of the tower would encumber their own sword arms. Smart eh?"

Although it made sense, Becket was more relieved to see that the old man had lowered his stick and continued to climb the winding, stone staircase.

"They were very shrewd, these medieval builders. If you look closely, every so often, one of the steps is either higher or wider than the others. These are known as trick or stumble steps. If you are dashing upstairs after your opponent you don't have time to look at your feet, so any change in pattern will make you stumble. Clever eh?"

Becket had noticed the steps were narrow even for his feet and each of his trainers easily sat over the edge of the stairs.

"Back in the Middle Ages," the old man explained, "people didn't live as long as we do now. Their poor diets and terrible hygiene meant they did not grow as big and tall as we do today."

At last they reached the top of the tower and walked out onto the roof, which gave a panoramic view of York below. Below them Becket could see the ruins of the old abbey, and a windmill in the distance. He strained his eyes, thinking he may even be able to see Swinford Manor on the horizon. When he looked down at the square below, he was relieved to his bike leaning up against the black railings.

"So Becket, how do you like the old Minster? I'm guessing that you are on your summer holiday? What else have you got planned?"

Becket explained about his parents and his aunt.

"Well my boy, don't ever forget the past. It's important to remember where you have come from in order to work out where you are going. But I have the feeling that you have been here before, my boy. I can tell these things. You have your whole life ahead of you," the old man enthused.

Becket thought he sounded like his aunt and why was a total stranger so keen to lecture him on the lessons of life.

"Anyway, enough of my melancholy musings, are you ready to tackle the stairs again? It's a long way back down and if we don't hurry the tourists will be struggling up and block our path."

As they descended, the old man floated ahead, seemingly untroubled by the narrow winding staircase. Becket began to feel a little giddy, slowing to steady himself. When he reached the bottom, the old man was nowhere to be seen. Becket scanned the Minster, but he had completely disappeared. A tour guide, checking a tour group's tickets, looked up at him in surprise and gave him a rude stare.

"There are two-hundred and seventy-five steps," the guide warned a group of aged Americans.

Wandering past the Quire Screen, Becket looked around. But there was no sign of the old man. How mental! Where had he gone? Maybe he was outside in the fresh air catching his breath.

He hurried through to the gift shop on his way to the exit and scanned the busy square. But there was still no sign of him. Becket turned back into the shop. He had time on his hands, so began to nose through the shelves at the usual tourist trappings. He leafed through the glossy brochures and looked vacantly at the post cards. Smiling at the small wooden swords and knight's outfits, remembering his younger days, Becket suddenly spotted on the front of a hardback book on the bottom shelf something remarkable. He bent down for a closer look.

It was a drawing of an ancient amulet and it bore an incredible likeness to his pendant. Becket grabbed the book: *Ancient History of York.*

It looked uninspiring, but leafing through, he scrutinised the photographs and drawings. Annoyingly couldn't find any similar to the one on the front cover.

I wonder if my pendant is valuable after all. Maybe it once belonged to an ancient Saxon king.

Becket took the book to a tall red-faced lady behind the counter. "How much is this please?'

The lady smiled and seemed amused. "What are you wanting with that old book? School project is it?"

Becket rattled the few coins he had left.

"On the basis it's been there for years, I guess I can give you a good discount. Give me 50p and it's all yours. Be glad of the shelf space, to be honest."

Becket handed her the coins and walked back into the Minster. Finding a cushioned stool in one of the pews, he opened the book and searched for information on the pendant. There it was, the drawing from the cover. The ancient amulet, it seemed had been found on an archaeological dig at York Castle. On closer inspection it was very similar, but not identical. When it had been examined and tested it was found to have originated from the Middle East. There seemed to be some speculation that it could be traced to the Knights Templar who had been tried in the Chapter House of the Minster for heresy in the early 1300s. Possibly part of the booty that was supposedly recovered by the saintly knights from the Temple on Solomon's Mount.

Becket had never heard of the Knights Templar, but they sounded like ancient superheroes - sort of priests with swords. The book didn't shed any further light, so he sat back, suddenly tired. His eyes felt heavy as he looked down at his own pendant. He would show his aunt the book. She would know its history. Becket yawned and rested his eyes as the Minster bell chimed four.

Becket started. The book had fallen to the floor and landed on his toe. He must have dropped off. Picking it up, he stashed it into his satchel and rushed down the aisle toward the far end of the cathedral. It had been a brief sleep, but full of vivid images. Scenes of knights on mighty steeds, of men fighting fiercely on battlements, of loud and colourful tournaments with beautiful maidens in long flowing dresses, noblemen in shiny amour and soldiers with large pikes controlling excited crowds of laughing, shouting people. Becket had never had such dreams. It seemed so very real, as if he had actually been there.

Becket sat down on a wooden chair in front of The Quire Screen. He looked down at the floor noticing the maze-like pattern of black stone winding a chaotic path through the white limestone floor. It would be great fun to whizz around the aisles on his bike following the trail as if he was on a madcap racetrack. The smoothness of the flagstones would make for a great ride.

The bellowing organ disturbed his thoughts. Becket wiped his dripping nose on the sleeve of his hoodie; it was cold in the cathedral. His eyes were drawn again to the line of statues of the ancient kings, their blank eyes staring past him, suspended in time. They had an almost god-like aura with their wild curly hair, holding their short swords and sceptres. On their heads sat golden crowns, a glimpse of the gaudy colours that had once adorned them. Above their crowns, like a futuristic halo, golden rapier-like spikes shot out, like mini-spaceships shooting them to heaven. He started to count and walked over for a closer look, reading the Latin names as he strolled along the screen. William the Conqueror was one of the few that he recognised. There was a King Stephen - he had a shorter robe than the others - and then a few spaces along was King Richard the First, the Lion heart, the man who one way or another had changed Becket's life forever. Next to him was King John; he of Robin Hood infamy, his head turned in Becket's direction, looking down at him with a frown almost like a schoolteacher telling-off a naughty pupil. The ancient queue continued on the other side of the dividing arch. There was Edward II, who seemed to be inspecting his fingernails, and Richard II had the maddest hair of them all; a mess of curls poking out to the side like a crazy cartoon character. The organ music continued to blare out and

Becket sat down, feeling a little giddy. He twisted his pendant between his fingers and stared at the ancient statues. They were captivating, frozen in time on their stone perches.

As he looked along the line, absent-mindedly counting the kings, he scratched his head. There were sixteen statues! Weren't there were only supposed to be fifteen? He must have miscounted, but after carefully recounting there were definitely sixteen. It was a mystery. This was silly, but then as he looked closer, he was startled to see a statue standing next to the Henry VI at the far right. Becket was sure it hadn't been there before. Becket's face began to colour. It didn't make sense. There had to be a logical explanation, but there it was, another stone king staring mournfully into the cathedral. Becket felt a fiery sensation on his chest and looking down at his pendant, he hastily withdrew his fingers.

"Ow!"

It was red-hot. The large ruby-like stone seemed darker, its colour deeper, more striking than ever. It had begun to throb and glow fiercely. Becket was frightened. The new statue seemed to be staring at him, its eyes ablaze. Becket was breathing hard, his left leg shaking uncontrollably. His arms felt like they were sprouting small pimples, the nerve ends rushing to exit his body. A red light arrowed out of the statue's lifeless eyes of the new king, burning into him. The pendant was growing hotter and hotter. The organ music louder and louder, almost deafening him. The light was blinding, Becket's head was spinning - the stone floor tilting as he gripped the arms of the chair. He had to look away, he wanted to run, but he was trapped. There was no escape; his head began to whirl, everything a blur and he was losing his balance – falling, spiralling downward, sinking further and further into an ever-deepening blackness, until all was still and silent.

CHAPTER 5

THE TOWER

Becket's head was pounding. He forced open his eyes and flinched at the dazzling sun. Scratching his itchy arms, the haze began to clear. A low hum of voices, indistinct, floated around him and just for a moment he had the feeling that he was back in his bedroom, at his aunt's house with the stifling odour of her concoctions filling the room - because he could smell something awful.

Becket looked around him. He was standing in the middle of a crowd of people all dressed in medieval clothing, as if they were taking part in a fancy dress pageant. This wasn't the Minster; it didn't even look like York. He remembered feeling strange and dizzy, but how had he got here? There were hundreds of people, chatting and laughing, many soldiers, sitting on horseback, watching the crowd. Horse-drawn carts passed by carrying fruits and vegetables, and yet more soldiers stood on the fringes of the crowd keeping them moving forward with the occasional swipe of their large wooden batons. Possibly some kind of medieval festival? But the costumes seemed ragged and dirty, unlike fancy-dress costumes. He choked as the stench grabbed him by the throat again.

Nobody took much notice of him as he was carried along in the throng. In the distance, there was a castle and behind it numerous boats speckled a wide, dirty brown river.

Becket was confused. Where on earth am I? The castle was vast and impressive. It couldn't be York. Hadn't the guidebooks said that only the ruins of the keep remained?

He studied the boats as they struggled against the current of a river that was far too wide to be the Ouse. He skidded on something slimy, thankful to his trainers for keeping him upright, and realised as he drew nearer to the castle that the stink came from the rubbish-filled moat. The crowd continued to jostle him along, and Becket frowned. In the centre of the castle, looming over the outer battlements, were four distinct towers with ornate black spires.

They were unmistakable: it had to be the Tower of London with the Norman White Tower sitting at its centre. He had only visited it last Christmas, ice-skating with his parents on the very spot where the moat now sat. But how could it be? He knew that the moat hadn't been used for hundreds of years. However important the occasion, they wouldn't have gone to all the effort to fill it - and more importantly, how had he travelled to London? He had been in York, at the Minster, sitting in front of the Quire Screen looking at the stone statues.

He fiddled with his long locks, as he was hustled along by the press of the crowd toward an arched gateway leading to a walkway into the main castle. He looked at the horizon, realising something was very wrong.

Where were all the tall modern buildings?

The far side of the river had a low skyline of short wooden houses, and beyond them, green fields as far as the eye could see. To his left in the place he knew Tower Bridge should be standing tall and proud, was just the dirty river full of boats.

Where were all the tourists, cameras in hand, munching on the supposedly "traditional fish and chips"?

A distant roar made him jump.

That sounded like a lion!

But Becket was no longer sure of anything. If this was a dream it was getting more bizarre by the minute.

"Buy a lovely pie, dearie?"

Becket ignored a tatty old woman shuffling along at the edge of the crowd. She was bent double from the weight of two baskets filled with pies and pasties. A couple of men stopped to buy some, stuffing them into their pockets without losing their place in the crowd.

"Mackerel, fresh mackerel," a fat-faced woman shouted.

"Fresh! Stinking more like!" muttered a man.

"I'll take four sheep's feet," said another man taking some coins from a leather purse and handing them over to a young girl, who looked no older than Becket.

Sheep's feet! Who eats sheep's feet?

To the barking cries of the street sellers, the crowd pressed forward onto a wooden drawbridge while the soldiers looked on for any sign of a disturbance. Although short of stature they looked strong and mean and Becket made sure he kept his distance. Another roar thundered out - that was definitely a lion.

No one else seemed concerned and the crowd just plodded on.

To the side of the drawbridge, Becket saw children throwing rotten fruit and vegetables at a man trapped in stocks. His head and hands were locked into holes in a horizontal wooden plank and his feet were similarly ensnared in a parallel plank below.

Luckily the children's aim wasn't good and the missiles sailed over his head or dropped short, exploding in the dust.

"Please set me free. I done nothing wrong. Help me."

The crowd laughed as a mouldy pear splatted into his face and hair, making the man wail all the more.

"Cease that noise," scolded one of the soldiers. "Be thankful that you weren't branded or had your ears cropped."

Becket forced his gaze away from the man and stepped onto the wooden drawbridge.

The soldiers continually prodded the crowd, "Keep moving. Move on there! You're holding up the others!"

The man to Becket's right shuffled along, eyes fixed ahead. He wore a baggy brown beret and his clothes were made of rough cloth. He smelled awful and had very few teeth left in his long, scarred face.

"Are we in York? Is this some sort of special festival or celebration?" Becket asked timidly.

The man spat noisily on the cobbled floor, "York? We be in London at the great Tower, you young fool. Are you not from these parts? Or mebbe you've been taking too much strong ale?"

So he was in London. It wasn't possible.

"York, you say," snarled the man, again displaying his peg-like teeth. "Are you one of those northern scum in the pay of the new King?"

There were angry murmurs from the crowd and people began to push and shove. Becket wasn't sure how to reply, but as he was funnelled through yet another gate and into the castle he was thankfully separated from the man. They had reached the main square and all the people rushed off leaving Becket standing alone looking up at the stone battlements. A young girl, a little older than him, dressed in sackcloth smiled at him. The soldiers were still yelling out orders and herding people into groups. Anyone too slow was struck with long wooden clubs. He was frightened. This wasn't just a dream, it was very real and he didn't like it one bit.

The girl walked over to him and grabbed him by the arm.

"Don't loiter here or the soldiers will notice and it will be the worse for you. Are you new here? What job have you come to do?" she whispered.

Becket looked at the girl. She was pretty, with a round, freckled face, flushed cheeks, large blue eyes and long, thick auburn hair that tumbled over her shoulders and onto her back.

"I have no idea where I am," he said.

The girl tugged at Becket's arm. "Come with me. Hurry up!"

She hurried off in the direction of one of the groups and Becket turned to follow her, but bumped into a scrawny man wearing a soiled black velvet suit and brown cloak. "Get out of my way you little fool. You need to take more care of where you're walking."

He had a thin face, thinning lank hair, and his yellow stumpy teeth protruded over his bottom lip causing him to lisp. A whiff of rank breath made Becket take a step back, causing him to bump into a finely dressed man standing behind him.

"Fool, out of my way…" the man began before faltering.

He ordered the first man, "Take care of this young ingrate Forest. Explain to him that he should bow when in the presence of a duke; otherwise he may find himself on a trip to Tyburn. A tight rope around his scraggy neck may make him remember his manners?"

"I am very sorry, Your Grace," interjected the man called Forest. "I will make sure he sees the error of his ways and that he learns how to behave in front of the Duke of Buckingham."

He grasped Becket's arm roughly, making him cry out.

The Duke wore a scarlet cloak with a heavy gold chain and locket sitting on the chest of his velvet tunic. Hiding most of his wispy hair was a beret decorated with a gold brooch. Becket had never seen a man dripping in so much gold. He looked and sounded every inch a duke and his lazy, sleepy eyes held a confidence that can only come with being born to power, money and influence.

"What manner of dress is this Forest? Perchance he is a foreigner from the Lowlands, or perhaps another Woodville spy here to try and help the royal brats."

"Possibly, Your Grace," simpered the tall man, "Shall I throw him in the dungeon for questioning?"

The man laughed and gripped Becket's sore arm even tighter.

"God's truth, Forest, do what you must, but make haste, I have much business to conclude."

Becket gulped. He felt close to tears. He never cried, not even on that fateful Sunday when he had been summoned to the head-master's office to be informed of his parents' deaths. How he wished he were with them now, living their humdrum life in their little terraced house.

Forest forced his head down toward the cobbled floor. Becket cried out in pain. The man smirked and was just about to drag him off, when from across the square a voice called, "Your Grace, please leave this boy to me."

The Duke peered at the man who had spoken. "Brackenbury, what business is this of yours? This boy means no good. You can tell as much by just looking at him. All matters of security are my jurisdiction and I won't be questioned."

Into Becket's view came a man with long silver hair that was swept back from his face. He had a thin silver moustache and a goatee. Becket noticed the girl with auburn hair hiding behind.

"I understand fully Your Grace," the grey haired man replied. "But I am Constable of the Tower and all business within its walls comes under my authority. I report directly to King Richard and to him alone."

"How dare you question me, Brackenbury? I am in command of this city while King Richard is on progress and I will deal with this dog as I see fit."

"Yes, Your Grace, but this young girl can vouch for him. She says he is her cousin from the north and is not used to our customs here in London - I can assure you he will learn them very quickly."

Forest looked at the Duke hopefully, still twisting Becket's arm. After a lengthy pause the Duke gathered his cloak and said, "Let him go Forest. We have more important matters to deal with."

Forest slackened his grip on Becket's sore arm and pushed him roughly to the ground.

"Be very clear Brackenbury, if this young cur crosses my path again I'll have him thrown into the dungeons where he will rot along with all the other Woodville spies." The Duke marched away with Forest hurrying after him.

The man called Brackenbury looked Becket up and down.

"Come with me young man. I have some questions for you. It looks like you could use a drink and a place to compose yourself." He then looked at the girl. "Thank you Bess, but I fear his lordship won't forget your part in this business. Go to your duties in the kitchen."

Bess half-smiled at Becket and hurried off. Two soldiers appeared at Becket's side and led him through a courtyard and a well-manicured garden and into a room with a low beamed ceiling. Brackenbury sat behind a large desk covered with scrolls of paper and piles of leather-bound books.

He smoothed his hair back. "You are a lucky young man. If Bess hadn't come to fetch me when she did, the Duke would have locked you in the dungeons and thrown away the key, or worse, chucked you into the Thames for the fish to feed on."

Becket fiddled with his hair. The man who sat in front of him must have been about his father's age, but his tired eyes made him seem much older. He eyed Becket closely, as if he had a notion that he had met him before.

"I am Sir Robert Brackenbury. It is your good fortune that I am Constable of the Tower of London. The Duke of Buckingham is welcome to believe what he wishes, but I have total authority here in the Tower. Now tell me, who are you and where you hail from?"

Becket eyed the soldiers standing either side of him. Bracken-bury, noticing his look, ordered them away with a dismissive wave.

"Your attire is most unusual. I have never seen such clothes. You do not dress like any Lowlander or Spaniard I have ever seen."

Becket didn't know what to say. This couldn't be happening to him. It made no sense. Either this was some sort of sick dream and he would wake up relieved in his bed or he had somehow been transported back in time. It was impossible, but seemed very real.

"Silence will get you nowhere. You need to trust me, young man. I can help you - but I need honest answers or I'm afraid it will be my duty to inform the King and he may decide to place you behind bars for more intensive questioning."

Brackenbury sighed. He looked exhausted.

Becket sat with his own shoulders slumped. Please wake up, he willed himself. Please be a dream.

"My name is Becket Bramble," he heard himself murmur. "I'm not from the Lowlands, wherever that is. I'm not from the north and I'm not a spy. I'm from England, just not from…here!"

Brackenbury stood up and paced around room.

"The cleanliness of your clothes, your fine teeth and hair suggest that you hail from an affluent family. Indeed you have a noble bearing. You bear a close resemblance to our royal princes that reside here in the Tower. By chance, have you run away from home?"

Becket felt numb, drained. His body an army of jabbing needles.

Brackenbury pushed a blank scroll, quill pen and some ink toward Becket. "Can you write, young fellow?"

Becket found himself picking up the pen. His hand unsteady and began to scratch his name on the rough parchment. The ink created a mess of blotches.

"Hmm, it is as I thought. You obviously have some learning and such a holy name, young sainted Becket," chuckled Brackenbury, "after our famous saint, Thomas à Becket, the Archbishop of

Canterbury. Poor devil was murdered for his faith. Well, if you get in the Duke's way again, the same fate may lay in store for you."

Brackenbury opened one of the books on the desk, turning the pages and became engrossed in the contents. He walked over to a small lead-framed window. Becket sat on his hands. He wasn't going to wake up, safe in his aunt's house. It wasn't a dream it was a nightmare. His eyes wandered to the book. It appeared to be some sort of accounts ledger. There were lots of columns with small figures all scrawled in wavy handwriting and as he looked up, he saw Brackenbury looking down at him.

"So you can read as well as write young fellow. I don't think you're a spy. You obviously have your own reasons for keeping the truth from me, but you must realise that I cannot help you if you do not confide in me. I'm sure you do not want to languish in the dungeons?"

Becket realised he would have to try to explain. How on earth could he even begin his unbelievable tale? He could hardly say that with the aid of a mystical pendant, he had travelled back in time hundreds of years.

"I told you. I'm from here but…just not from now. I don't know how I came to be here. I'm not a spy! I have no idea who I'm supposed to spying on." Becket choked back the panic that was rising through him.

Brackenbury drummed his fingers on the desk. "Young man, I would like to help you, but you are asking me to believe that you have no knowledge of the two royal princes that live here in the Tower?" He handed Becket a linen cloth to dry his eyes. "They have been kept here since the late king, their father, died and their mother the Queen fled to the sanctuary in Westminster Abbey. King Richard has placed them here under my jurisdiction for their safety and for the security of the realm."

"I don't know anything about princes and kings. I have no idea why I am here or even how I got here."

"It's such a responsibility and one that I wish had never been thrust upon me,"

Brackenbury continued, almost as if he had forgotten Becket was in the room. "The boys are just pawns in a fight for supremacy. There are those who would like to control them and make Edward king. There are others, powerful people, who would see the boys come to harm in order to further their own claims to the throne."

Brackenbury looked out of the window.

"These are turbulent and troubled times, Becket. I would be happier if King Richard were back in London and not heading to York on the royal progress. I do not trust anyone, least of all the mighty Duke of Buckingham."

Becket looked dubiously at the leather tankard set in front of him.

"I'm afraid I have no fine wine, young man, but I am sure you will find the small beer will help steady your nerves and quench your thirst."

Becket had never heard of small beer – he couldn't believe he was being offered alcohol.

Brackenbury looked amused as Becket attempted to sip the light brown liquid. He was thirsty, but found it very bitter and it burned his throat as he forced it down.

"Well. I don't know what's to be done with you, young fellow. God knows I would like to help. Too many of our young people are suffering in these times. Too many are reduced to crimes that lead to the gallows."

Then Brackenbury, a wide smile lighting up his furrowed face said, "Perhaps I could use you. You are of the same age. You obviously have some education and the benefit of being untouched by the corrupt factions scrabbling for their favour. I think the idea has merit – yes it may work."

Brackenbury pulled at his clipped beard.

"How would you like to help me? The princes could do with another page and I need somebody who will be loyal to me and close to the two boys: somebody who can be my eyes and ears and who can warn me at the first sign of mischief. Would you help me, young fellow?" he said resting his hands on Becket's shoulders.

"As the boys page, you would stay with them day and night and therefore be in the perfect place to warn me of any danger."

Becket's head was swimming. He felt like he hadn't slept for weeks. The enormity of his horrendous predicament just wouldn't sink in. It was so unreal.

"Becket, you will be doing not only me, but also your King a great service and I promise I will do the utmost help you find your way home."

Becket put his hand to his forehead, "I don't understand how I got here and I'm sure I can't be much help. All I really want is to find a way to get back home."

He was scared and confused. Should he trust this man? Did he have any choice? What else was he going to do?

"Our friend the Duke of Buckingham controls those that serve and monitors those that visit. I realise I am asking much, but to have you on the inside would be a great benefit." Before Becket could protest, Brackenbury went to the door.

"Don't worry. I will get Black Will to show you the ropes. He's a little simple, but means well."

He shouted to the soldiers to fetch Bess from the kitchens.

"Bess can find you a place to sleep tonight and will fetch you some food. You can start on the morrow."

Moments later Bess entered the room, and Becket stood up.

"Don't let me down, Becket. Be vigilant and trust no one. I'm relying on you."

Bess and Becket were ushered out of his office and Becket found himself once more standing in the flagged square of the Tower of London, the four familiar towers looking down on him.

Bess smiled at him shyly. "Impressive isn't it? The grandest and tallest building in the city. What is your name? Your clothes are strange, but most becoming."

"My name's Becket. It's hard for me to explain where I'm from and even harder to know how I get back there."

"What curious shoes you wear. I have never seen the like of them before."

He looked down at his trainers, sweatshirt and jeans painfully aware that he looked out of place. He took a closer look at the girl. She was shorter than him by some inches with a freckled face and full red lips. He felt easy in her company, almost as if he had known her from somewhere before. But that was impossible.

Bess noticed him studying her and started walking toward a wooden building, beckoning him to follow.

"The barn is the best place to sleep within the castle. It is warm and comfortable and the straw makes a snug bed even if you have to share it with the odd rat. I will make sure something is brought from the kitchens for your supper before I leave."

"Leave? I thought maybe you lived and worked here?"

"I do work here, but like most, I leave before curfew. When the evening bell sounds I have to get home to see to supper for my father and brother. I have been looking after them ever since my mother died two years ago. I am lucky to have this position and Sir Robert has been kind to me. I was badly treated by the soldiers when I first arrived, but he has looked after me ever since."

Bess seemed smart. Becket managed a faint smile.

"Thank you for saving me from those two men. If you hadn't arrived when you did…"

"Be very careful, Becket. The tall, skinny man is Forest. He is cruel and a bully and likes nothing better than inflicting pain on those smaller and weaker than him. He is manservant to the Duke of Buckingham, the second most powerful man in the land after the king. Keep out of their way if you can."

He heard yet another muffled roar. "Isn't that a lion?"

"Of course it's a lion," Bess laughed. "We have many here at the Tower. They live in the cages under the main gate. There are many exotic creatures here: monkeys, leopards, there was even a polar bear once!"

Becket thought of his visits to the zoo at Colchester and his disappointment as the bored, lacklustre lions snoozed in the sun.

"Do you not have such animals in your land?" Bess asked.

"In my time, Bess, they are kept in large pens in places we call zoos."

"In your time?"

"Yes, as I keep trying to tell everyone, I come from here, but many years from now! I'm not from some foreign land, but from England many hundreds of years in the future and I'm definitely not a spy."

He instantly regretted his outburst as he could see he had offended Bess.

"Well, I understand if you must conceal the secrets of your life, but I wouldn't go around telling folk hereabouts such tales unless you want to be burned as a witch," she replied.

They had reached the barn, and despite the biting smell of animal urine, it looked a comfortable place to sleep.

"Will I see you tomorrow?" he asked Bess.

Bess pulled back her long auburn locks up into a ponytail and strode off in the direction of the kitchen, shouting back, "You may. I will be in the kitchens as usual. Black Will should come for you in the morning and show you your duties. Good night, strange Becket."

He hated to see her go. He didn't want to be left alone, but making himself a makeshift bed out of the bales of straw, he lay down - his mind full of questions. He wished his dad were here. He would have known what to do. He would have been so excited to be alive in medieval England. His stomach rolled uncontrollably as he tried to contain his fear. How was he going to get home? He looked down at his swinging pendant. If only his aunt had told him about its frightening power. What right had she to tell him to wear it always without a warning? Was she mad? It was a nightmare: his parents' death, Aunt Lizzie and her scary house in the wood, the Minster and the nutty old man brandishing his stick as they climbed the tower. Perhaps if he went to sleep he would wake up in his old bed in the little terraced house and rush out to play on his bike. Tears dripped down onto the straw. He pushed at the pendant, but it was no good – the stupid thing had a mind of its own. He lay back on the scratchy straw and tried to sleep.

CHAPTER 6
THE TWO PRINCES

Becket awoke to a sharp jab to his ribs. He opened his bleary eyes and looked up at the wooden beams of the barn. The nightmare came rushing back. However unbelievable, he was in the Tower of London in medieval England. He felt helpless, but for the sake of his sanity, he would have to get on with it. A tall, skinny boy hovered over him. He looked like an over-sized raven, just like the many that inhabited the castle. Becket rubbed his eyes.

"Please, please get up! We shall be late and they will be sure to beat me," said the Raven.

Becket sat up, dusted the strands of straw from his clothes. The boy's pale white face topped with the most startling shock of the blackest hair he had ever seen, twitched and begged him again, "Please be quick. We need to hurry."

The boy was dressed entirely in black and even had a black handkerchief tied around his scraggy neck. This had to be Black Will!

The stars were shining in a dark sky. Surely it wasn't time to wake up.

"What time is it?" Becket asked with a yawn.

"Time? I know nothing of time," answered Black Will. "The princes are at prayer and we need to be waiting for them at their apartments. Make haste or we shall be in trouble."

Becket had little choice but to follow Will.

"Where are we going?" Becket asked, as he fought to smooth his long blond locks into some sort of order.

"To the Garden Tower where the two princes have been day and night these past six weeks. They barely see the light of day apart from the odd trip to the garden or the small chapel."

Black Will guided him down a cobbled causeway toward a squat rectangular tower. A wall of heat hit Becket as he followed Will into a candlelit room. There was a group of soldiers huddled around a large fireplace. Will led him past the winch that operated the portcullis below and they climbed a winding staircase. It was dark and Becket slipped several times on the narrow slimy stone steps. At the top, he was led into a sparsely furnished room, the floor of which was covered in rushes. To the centre of the room there was a table surrounded by some wooden chairs. Will hurried him along, through another doorway into a much more impressive room. This was evidently the princes' main apartment, as at one end of the room, next to the fireplace, was a four-poster bed shrouded in embroidered green curtains and covered with red and gold silk blankets.

In the middle of the room stood a long table covered with a white linen cloth and silver plates, platters and bowls all filled with meat, fruits and tarts. There were jugs of pale red wine and beer, and clean white linen napkins sat neatly at either end.

"This is where the princes will break their fast. You will help me serve them and make sure they have everything they need," stuttered Will. "I am so useless. I was never trained to serve at the table, but the Duke has sent away all their servants, leaving only me and their doctor to attend them."

Becket looked at the full jugs of wine.

"I am so clumsy I am sure I will make a mess of things and then the Duke will have Forest thrash me again," said Will, his face twitching in agitation.

Becket didn't like the idea of being beaten and he didn't have the heart to tell Will that he had never served at table. He studied the rest of the room - fine colourful tapestries depicting hunting and fishing scenes adorned the drab walls. Hundreds of flickering candles that gave the room a shadowy golden glow, and beneath his feet was a glazed, patterned tile floor. The lavish furnishings of the room suggested the importance of its occupants. Just as he was wondering what it would be like to sleep in such a grand bed the door opened and in walked two boys. A middle-aged man, bowing his head deferentially, keeping his distance followed them into the room, stopped behind one of the chairs at the head of the table.

The two boys ignored Becket and Will and sat down at either end of the long table. Although they were of similar height, one of the boys had a pallid complexion and shoulder-length, sandy hair and the other had much longer blond curls, similar to Becket's. In fact, the blond prince was almost Becket's double. He had the same long nose and lean pale face.

Becket could now see why the Duke had seemed confused and Brackenbury had been so keen to employ his services.

The boy with the sandy-coloured hair, who appeared to be the elder of the two, didn't seem very happy and looked at the food with distaste. Will picked up a large jug and attempted to poor some wine into his goblet, but poor Will's trembling hands spilt it all over the table.

"You clumsy oaf!" shouted the boy. "Why am I left with such a buffoon? Why can't I have my old servants from my castle at Ludlow? It's insufferable."

The second boy smiled at his brother cheerfully. "That's because, Edward, my dear brother, you are no longer destined to be king. Good old Uncle Richard has seen to that. I'm afraid that we have to become accustomed to our new life, as I suspect we may be here for some time."

Becket, noticing Will's obvious distress, wiped up the mess and hurriedly refilled the boys' goblets. The annoyed boy barely noticed, and picked distastefully at some chicken.

In contrast, the other boy chomped noisily on a full plate of food, and looking up at Becket asked, "So who are you then? Not another of the Duke's spies are you? Or maybe one of Morton's moles?"

He had no idea who Morton was, but was annoyed at being called a spy yet again.

"My name is Becket Bramble. I am here because that's what Sir Robert wanted and I am certainly not a spy!"

"Bit of spirit in this one, Edward," said the boy to his brother. "Take a closer look. You see the resemblance. He could be our brother. The same long Plantagenet nose and blond locks."

And turning to Becket, "Well, you are most welcome Becket Bramble. Maybe you will liven things up around here. God knows, life is so very dull being cooped up in this place day and night."

Becket looked over at the middle-aged man standing behind the table. He had a long brown beard that had a peculiar white tuft in the middle as if he had had an accident whilst painting. He had to be the doctor that Will had mentioned. Now he came forward and sniffed suspiciously at the boys' goblets, and then withdrew, nodding to Edward that it was all right to drink.

"Doctor, you fuss too much. Nobody is going to poison us. It's a little obvious don't you think?" said the younger boy, and turning to Becket continued,

"You appear to be new to this work and it seems obvious that you are not from these parts. I assume you have been informed who we are?"

Becket shook his head.

The boy gave him a look of distrust, but explained, "Well my name is Richard and my elder brother is Edward. Our dear father was King Edward."

Wolfing down another sticky fruit tart he continued, "Well you will have heard of our mother? Queen Elizabeth?"

Becket stood dumbly and waited for the boy to continue.

"I guess it's of no matter, but she hides herself away in the sanctuary at the great abbey in Westminster, along with our sisters, for fear our Uncle Richard, our newly crowned King of England, will have her imprisoned for treason. So you see that we, the unloved and unwanted, find ourselves caged here and will remain so, until our king decides what to do with us. I fear we are a nuisance that he wished didn't exist."

Becket wasn't that interested in the boy's story. All he wanted was for Brackenbury to help him get home. Maybe if he could get to York, to the Quire screen, then the pendant would reverse its magic and send him back to the twenty-first century. But he had to get back to York.

Edward did not appear to be listening and was nursing the right side of his face, wincing in pain.

"Doctor Argentine, please do something," he shouted. "I fear this ache in my teeth will be the end of me - I sometimes wish it were so."

"I'm sorry Your Highness, but I have asked for another batch of myrrh to ease your pain, but his grace the Duke has refused."

"What right has he to deny you? Have you informed Brackenbury?'

"I'm afraid he is too busy to grant me an audience. The Duke's physicians have sent me a basket of the dreaded henbane. They tell him that leeches and henbane are the best and only cure and that they will draw out the worms that infect your teeth. It's ridiculous! I'm afraid, Your Highness, that these inept fools are frauds and know little of the science of medicine. Worms indeed! These amateurs cause more damage than they cure, but until the Duke relents I'm afraid there is little I can do."

Richard wandered over and sniffed at a basket full to the brim with large green leaves and pale goblet-shaped flowers that were full of black seeds.

"Please keep away from there, Highness!" shouted the doctor. "To even inhale the scent of black henbane can make you light headed and possibly faint."

Richard quickly took a step back, covering his nose instinctively with an embroidered handkerchief, but seemed none the worse for the experience.

"I keep asking for the basket to be disposed of, but the Duke's physician insists the henbane must be administered. I will never acquiesce; I have heard of many instances where it has caused great harm. There was a case in the Lowlands where a doctor burned the seeds and inhaled the fumes. He began to see fire-breathing beasts. His whole body became numb and it was said that he thought that he could fly. The plant is best avoided, so please keep away from it."

The doctor moved the basket to the window, covering it with a linen cloth. He looked up as Edward groaned again and pushed away his plate in annoyance. Will took this as a sign that breakfast was over and started to remove the plates.

Becket began to help, as Prince Richard scoffed yet another tart and explained to him, "Don't worry about my brother. He's always moaning and worrying about his teeth. Doctor Argentine is the best physician in England and we are very lucky he hasn't been spirited away like the rest of our servants. Lord knows what would happen if he were not here, as we wouldn't even be able to trust the food that we eat."

Despite Will's obvious awkwardness they soon had the table cleared and were dismissed from the room. The smell of the food reminded Becket of how hungry he was. He realised that he hadn't eaten since yesterday.

Will nibbled at an untouched pie and noticing Becket eyeing the food, said, "Take what you want, but be quick before the soldiers come. It's one of the perks of the job; we get first pickings of whatever food is left over."

Becket looked at Will's bony legs and arms and thought it was unlikely that he ate very much at all, and as disgusting as the thought of eating leftovers was, he devoured a large piece of chicken, whilst grabbing some small apples and stuffing them into the pockets of his hoodie.

After washing the breakfast things and resetting the table, they were told they wouldn't be needed until the princes took their morning exercise in the garden.

On reaching the lower floor, Black Will sat himself down on a window ledge and looked out of a narrow barred window at the river Thames below. The early morning breeze was hardly fresh, but a welcome change from the stifling room. Becket looked more closely at the odd-looking boy. His clothes were no more than rags and at least two sizes too small for him. His unkempt, greasy hair looked as if it had never seen a brush or comb.

"How long have you been here, Will?" Becket asked.

"Don't know. This place is all I have known."

"Don't you have any parents or brothers or sisters?"

"Never known no parents. Just me, on my own, although Sir Robert has been very good to me."

"I am on my own also," said Becket trying not to think about his own parents.

Will brightened a little.

"Perhaps you can be my friend and you can teach me not to be so... so...and m-maybe Forest won't hit me again?"

Becket playfully poked the taller boy in his skinny ribs in response.

As the sun broke over the Thames, hundreds of small boats appeared like a swarm of water insects scurrying on its surface.

"We must go to the princes now," said Will, abruptly jumping up from his perch on the windowsill like a giant bird readying itself for flight. "They will be ready for their morning exercise in the garden."

They again climbed the narrow winding staircase and found Prince Richard striding up and down the room, tugging at his elder brother's arm and grumbling.

"Oh come on Edward, don't be so dull. Please come outside and help me practice my swordsmanship. It will take your mind off your blasted teeth and I want to learn to be as fine a warrior as our father and old Uncle Rivers."

"It's all right for you, little brother," answered Edward, "but you are not plagued by this constant pain. I sometimes think it would be better for everyone - our uncle the King, the Duke, Lady Beaufort and her beloved cowardly son - if I were no more."

Edward sat with his head in his hands.

The brothers were so different. The melancholy Edward seemed older than his years; the energetic Richard was full of life and vigour, almost seemed to be the elder of the two. After much cajoling from his younger brother, Edward finally agreed to take some exercise in the garden which was situated conveniently just outside their apartments.

"Come on brother, it will be fun!" shouted Richard. "And we can see how Becket handles a sword and bow. He can't be as bad as the good doctor or lumbering old Will."

The soldiers standing guard in the room below followed them into the adjacent garden, where Richard immediately picked up a large wooden sword and shield and starting swishing, chopping and stabbing the air enthusiastically. Edward had seated himself under a large oak tree next to the entrance to the tower, and start-ed to read a small leather-bound book. Richard sighed,

"You're no fun, brother. I have been cooped up in the Abbey for a month with only our mother and sisters for company, and now I'm here all you do is sit and read your dull prayer book."

Richard picked up a second sword and shield and passing them to Becket said, "Come on Becket, show me what you are made of. I will fight for the House of York, you can be a dastardly Lancastrian."

Becket had no idea about being any sort of Lancastrian, but had little option but to agree as Richard charged at him waving his sword above his ahead and shouting a fierce battle cry. The young boy was so strong and fierce, Becket was thankful for the large wooden shield that took the brunt of the assault. Richard had been trained with the sword from a very young age. However hard Becket defended himself, Richard consistently breeched his defences with a thrust to the ribs or a chop to his thigh that made him wince with pain and was always followed by an ecstatic cry of "Hurrah for Saint George!"

Richard soon became tired of winning their duels and suggested that they try their hand with the longbow. Becket looked at the gi-gantic bow and wondered how he would have the strength to fire the weapon. Richard, however, was soon finding his target - another oak tree some fifty metres away with the long, sleek arrows. Becket couldn't help admiring his skill and thought he must have practised long and hard, as Becket himself had, shooting the endless baskets in the school gym. He would give anything to be back there now.

When it was his turn he found he barely had the strength to pull back the taut thick twine, and the arrows merely plopped to the ground or fell embarrassingly short of their target. Richard laughed at his pathetic attempts and Becket became frustrated and angry until finally pulling back the bow back with all his strength he fired the arrow high into the sky and up into the branches of the tree.

"Well, that's one arrow we shan't be shooting again," Richard chuckled. "Maybe we should think of a suitable penance or perhaps we should just stop your food and drink for a day or two."

Becket had heard enough. He jogged resolutely over to the tree and before the soldiers could stop him, shinned up high into the branches to retrieve the arrow, dropping back to the ground with a smile.

"Huzzah!" exclaimed Richard. "You climbed that tree like one of the apes in the menagerie."

He looked down admiringly at Becket's trainers.

"Those outlandish shoes that you wear must have been a great help.

I couldn't even climb a ladder in these useless things," he added, looking down at his own soft leather shoes.

Another expert bow and arrow display from Richard was interrupted by more protestations from the ailing Edward, so they finally went back inside, much to Richard's annoyance. Becket had enjoyed the fresh air and exercise. It had temporarily taken his mind off his situation and he was now depressed to be back in the muggy staterooms. What was he going to do? York seemed a million miles away. He would have to try and speak to Brackenbury when the chance allowed.

After another uneventful meal, where the unfortunate Will managed to smash a bowl of hot soup all over the tiled floor and the doctor's hose, much to Richard's amusement, it was once again time for the princes to go to prayer in the small chapel of St John in the White Tower. Becket couldn't remember the last time he had been to church. He thought people in medieval England spent a lot of time praying.

Will informed him that on the boys' return they would be required to attend their toilet, readying the princes for a long afternoon wading through the day's visitors' list. It was warming up outside and even the cold stone walls of the castle seemed to be losing their chill. Becket longed to be out in the fresh air, but after attending the princes on their tiresome and deliberate toilet, took his place dutifully behind them as they sat side by side at the table in the smaller anteroom. With the heat of the day, he soon became bored and sleepy. There was a constant flow of officials seeking the boys' signatures on endless bundles of scrolls of papers. The time seemed to drag in the stuffy room, reminding him of the dull, long afternoons in the ICT lessons where he'd longed for the bell that would signal the end of another school day.

Becket was disturbed from his daydreams, by the entrance of a short, pugnacious-looking lady marching into the room. On her head was a bizarre peaked hat that reminded him of the birdhouse in the garden at home. She was followed closely by a clergyman and an immaculately dressed, self-assured-looking man.

"I hope I find you both well, Your Highnesses?" said the lady as she curtseyed.

"Not particularly, Lady Beaufort," sniffled Edward.

"You know, Bishop Morton and my man Bray?"

The two men bowed respectfully. Becket looked at the lady. What a scary and sinister looking woman. She reminded him of the wicked witches from the old films such as *Snow White and The Seven Dwarves* and *The Wizard of Oz*. Her extraordinary white peaked hat framed her pale, wrinkled face and drooped down onto the shoulders of her grey gown. She looked like a nun or a sister in a convent. Her heavy-lidded, piercing black eyes, almost too large and out of place in her gaunt face, made her look like a giant bird of prey. Becket studied her as closely as he dare. There was something in the way that she held herself, an air of menace that made him think back to the day back in the woods and the shadowy figure at the window of the manor. She was creepy. Not the sort of woman to make an enemy of, he hastily looked away.

The clergyman's blinking eyes scanned the room, constantly rubbing his hands together as if washing them clean of some invisible grime.

"I have no time for pleasantries, Your Highness," said the lady. "I will come straight to the point. Your uncle, the King, has taken your throne and you are declared illegitimate. This much is obvious. It is an appalling circumstance that has befallen your family. I am most unhappy with the current state of affairs. My husband, Lord Stanley, as you are well aware is one of the most powerful barons in the land and with his brother William can muster the largest independent army in the country."

The clergyman's eyes burned into Edward's for a sign of a reaction, but the boy sat bravely and impassive.

"My son, Henry Tudor," she continued, tapping her foot impatiently, "is in exile in France. He has a strong claim to the throne of England through my great-great-grandfather."

Richard looked agitated and was about to speak when the well-dressed man said. "My Lady, let's not be hasty. We do not want to be accused of coercing His Highness with treasonable talk."

He spoke confidently and seemed a very capable man who knew how to get his own way. He had brown hair, a soft well-clipped beard and calm blue eyes.

"How dare you speak to me of treason, Bray!" the old lady shouted, her black eyes wide. "His Highness is well aware that his mother, Lady Elizabeth, is constantly scheming and striving in order to set him back on the throne."

Edward sat emotionless, making no reply.

The clergyman stepped forward alongside the old lady and said, "Your Highness, if I may be so bold. My Lady has the seeds, no more than seeds mind, of an idea."

He spoke breathlessly. He was dressed in a long scarlet robe with a matching beret and had an olive, fleshy face with a prominent nose and eyes that were rather too close together giving the impression that he was constantly looking at something curious in the distance.

"The idea," he continued, "with My Lady's permission, is this - your family support the claim to the throne of England of Henry Tudor, and in return we will arrange a marriage between your eldest sister Elizabeth and Henry on his accession."

Becket didn't like the look on the old lady's face. Her eyes burned pure hatred.

Richard could hold back no longer.

"How dare you suggest such a thing? My brother is the rightful King of England. Why would my family support your flimsy claim?"

The old lady interrupted,

"Listen to me. The King has declared you illegitimate. Your brother will never be king. You are both in a very hazardous position. Your uncle sees you as a nuisance and has no idea what to do with you. He is obviously aware that you may be used as powerful pawns in an uprising and there could be a revolt at any time. You need as many friends as you can get."

"Don't threaten us or I…" shouted Richard.

"You young fool. I don't know if you are aware, but your very lives hang by the slimmest of threads," spat the old lady. "You have been warned. Take heed. I will speak again with your mother on this matter, but I suggest that you give it very careful consideration before it is too late for the both of you."

She marched out of the room. Morton and Bray hurried after her, stopping briefly, to bow respectfully to the princes.

Becket puffed out his cheeks and let out a relieved low whistle as Richard jumped up from the table, his chair falling to the floor. Edward sat blankly and said nothing. He hadn't moved except to occasionally rub the side of his face gingerly.

"How dare they? We should inform the King and let him deal with them," shrieked Richard.

"Brother," Edward said, finally speaking. "Our uncle is on royal progress and there is no way to get a message to him. Even if we could, he wouldn't believe us. It's not in his interest to upset the Stanleys. Lady Beaufort makes an obvious point. We have many enemies and our position is indeed a precarious one. I have no energy to discuss this further. The pain is too much. I should like to lie down." He got up from the table. "How I wish I was at Ludlow with faithful Uncle Rivers, but alas he is no more. Perchance I will see him soon – perhaps in a more peaceful place."

He then waved dismissively to Becket and Will and walked slowly out of the room and into the bedchamber.

Becket was relieved to once again find himself outside in the sunshine, leaving Will in his favourite spot sitting at the window, watching the boats on the river.

Shaken, Becket wandered through the gardens toward the kitchens, hoping for a sight of Bess. He feared the evil-looking lady really meant to get her way one way or another. For some reason he couldn't get the shadowy figure from the manor out of his head.

The thought of meeting Bess again, cheered Becket. He yawned noisily as he walked down the stone steps that led into the basement kitchen. The heat of the room hit him as he walked toward a large table in the centre of the room where several men in aprons were preparing food. Becket instantly spotted Bess's auburn head at the far side of the room, next to an enormous fireplace, where meats were roasting on long spits. She was peeling vegetables from a barrel of water, seemingly unworried by the fierce heat of the fire. Nobody seemed very interested in him as he wandered over.

Her face was red from the heat.

"You are still here then? They haven't burned you as a witch?" she teased.

The heat from the fire was almost unbearable and the fat from the meat spat at them.

"Yes, I'm still here," he replied. "Black Will has managed to keep me out of trouble."

Bess's red, chafed hands looked very sore, but she carried on peeling.

"I suppose it must be time for you to go home soon?" he asked.

"Yes, my father and brother will be waiting for their supper."

She seemed to lead a very tough life for such a young girl. A long hard day working at the castle followed by more of the same when she reached home.

"My father is a tanner," she explained, "and my brother is following in his footsteps. It is a very hard life skinning and staining cow hides all day. My father is becoming a bit too old. I'm afraid he has never got over the death of my dear mother."

"What happened to her?"

"She died of the flux," murmured Bess. "One day she caught a fever and had cramps; the next day she was dead. My father blamed himself. He said that the disease was spread from the cowhides, but many people were taken. They say it was from the bad water. It wasn't his fault."

She looked down at the floor and wiped a sore, wet hand across her hot brow.

"Well, he's lucky to have you," Becket said.

Bess smiled.

"I'm lucky to have this job, and until my brother Tom finds himself a wife, I will continue to keep house for them as best I can."

"Bess, do you know how I could get to York? I know it's very far, but I need… "

He was interrupted by a sniggering voice from behind them.

"Maybe you should think about getting yourself married, my pretty Bess?"

They turned round to see Forest, lounging against the wall and leering at Bess.

"I've asked you many a time and you know you only have to say the word and I'm all yours," he smirked.

"Miles Forest, I'd rather marry the devil himself than be wed to the likes of you."

"Don't be like that Bess, you know you love me really and we would make such a great match with your beauty and my brains. I'm sure your father would think that I was a great catch eh?" he laughed, pulling her towards him and grabbing her around the waist.

"Let go of me you pig!" Bess screamed as she struggled to release herself.

She turned her head from side to side, trying to avoid his kisses.

"Just hold still wench," Forest continued, becoming more and more frustrated and annoyed.

Becket could watch no longer and picked up a poker from beside the fireplace, whacking Forest across the back of his legs.

"*Aaaaarghh!*"

He released his hold on Bess, turned and clawing at Becket, slipped on some vegetable peelings and landed in a heap on the floor, banging his head on a table. Several of the workmen began to laugh and Forest got up, rubbing his head, aimed a kick at a stool. He screamed in pain and hopped across the floor holding his injured foot.

"You'll live to regret that, you little foreign spy," he shouted, and stumbled out of the kitchen, to the sound of even more laughter from the kitchen workers.

Becket started to laugh and was surprised when Bess scolded him, "You shouldn't have done that. You will be in big trouble when he tells his master the Duke. I fear, Becket, he will want his revenge."

Becket stopped laughing. She was probably right. The evening bell tolled and Bess took him by the arm and led him out of the kitchen into the cool summer evening. Becket felt elated. Perhaps it was because he had stood up to the bully or maybe because Bess held onto him so tenderly. He liked the feeling. He had never had his arm held by a girl before. They both laughed at the thought of Forest hopping around the kitchen.

"York you say, Becket? I fear that is very far from here and even if you had a horse, the roads are too dangerous and it would take days, maybe weeks to get there. Is that where you hale from?"

She was interrupted by a booming voice from across the causeway.

"Stop that boy! Stop him at once in the name of the King!"

They turned and saw the Duke striding towards them with Forest dragging along behind.

Two soldiers grabbed Becket by his arms and hauled him towards the Duke. Bess melted into the crowd as it slowly pushed its way toward the exit of the great Tower.

The Duke looked down at him with a sneer, "I warned you not to be brought to my attention again, boy. I have been told that you attacked my man," he went on. "I consider it an attack on my person and therefore treason."

"Take him to the dungeons. A night in a dark cell with only the rats for company may loosen that lying tongue of his. I shall deal with him in the morning."

The soldiers marched Becket back through the gate of the Garden Tower, dragging his feet on the rough stones as they went. He was pushed down a dark, staircase, into the bowels of the castle and thrown inside a cell.

The room was pitch-black. It stank of damp and decay. The only sound breaking the blackness was the scurrying feet of rats. Becket had never been afraid of rodents, but he prayed there were no spiders. The situation was hopeless. He banged his hands repeatedly on the door and yelled, "Let me out of here. I'm not a spy, let me out of here."

It was pointless. He rested his head against the cold wall and started to sob. Would he never get to York? He hated medieval

England. He tried to remember what his dad had tried to teach him. How he wished he had listened more carefully.

Just as he was thinking he might as well try and get some much needed sleep, a thought came to him. How stupid he had been. King Richard, two princes kept locked up in the Tower of London. The Houses of Lancaster and York. He remembered watching a TV programme with his dad about one of the greatest mysteries in the history of Britain: The Princes in the Tower. King Richard had taken the throne from his nephew, Edward, and had sent the two brothers to the Tower supposedly for safekeeping. One day they were there, and then, they had just seemed to vanish and were never seen again. Nobody had seemed to care or make much of a fuss and King Richard had died not long afterwards, fighting in battle for his throne. Becket remembered Shakespeare had written a play about it. It had been assumed at the time that their uncle, King Richard, had done away with the young boys although the bodies had never been found. The mystery of the Princes in the Tower's disappearance was never solved until centuries later two small skeletons had been found in a chest buried in a disused stairway deep within the Tower. Although it was never proven, it was assumed that they were the bodies of the princes, and their remains were interned in Westminster Abbey alongside the many other kings and queens of England. Rubbing his temple, as if to coax an idea out of his brain, Becket shivered. Edward and Richard were in grave danger. But what could he do? He had no idea how to escape nor what the Duke had in store for him, but he had to find a way to warn the two boys before it was too late.

CHAPTER 7

SANCTUARY

Two hands grabbed Becket, shaking him.
"Come on, Becket - make haste! We need to be gone from here."

It was freezing and everything ached. He had barely slept.

"Becket, get up – hurry! We cannot dally any longer."

His feet were numb; his hands had pins and needles. He stumbled up after two hazy figures and out into crisp morning air. He was led across the garden and was soon sitting in Brackenbury's office. The old man peered at him with a look of concern, "Are you all right, Becket? Have some small beer. It'll make you feel better."

A leather cup was pushed towards him.

Becket drank, the beer burning the back of his throat. His hands trembled and he rubbed his arms, warming himself as his head eventually began to clear.

Brackenbury said, "Becket, you are a very lucky boy. If Will hadn't seen you being dragged off, you would still be locked away in that frightful place."

Becket noticed Black Will standing behind him.

"I feel responsible for having placed you in such a dangerous situation. The Duke had no right to imprison you without my permission. I fear his power and influence grow daily with the King no longer in London. I worry what he may do next."

Brackenbury paced up and down, his hands clasped behind his back.

"What were you thinking of Becket? I heard you attacked his man. What were you doing in the kitchen? You had no business in being there."

Becket was about to explain about Forest and his attack on Bess when Brackenbury carried on, "It's of no consequence. What's done can't be undone. We just need to get you back into the safety of the state apartments as soon as possible before the Duke realises you have been released. You will be safe there."

He looked out of the window.

"I thought I was helping by placing you in this position of trust, as much like Bess, you remind me of someone from my past." He clenched his fists, rubbed his chin and looked to the window. "A young girl, so long ago, dressed strangely, much like yourself, almost as if … not from another land, but a different world. She helped me…but it's of no matter. Time moves on."

He turned to face Becket.

"Please go back to the princes and stay out of the Duke's way."

This was his last chance.

"Sir Robert, you need to get the princes away from this place. They are in the most terrible danger. Something awful is going to happen if you don't act quickly," Becket pleaded.

"Move them from the Tower? That's impossible! The King would never sanction it. This is the safest place in the kingdom."

"But you must! They will come to great harm if you leave them where they are. Please, you must believe me!"

"Fie! Perhaps you could explain to me why you are so convinced that the boys are in such danger."

Brackenbury turned to Will and dismissed him from the room. Becket managed a grateful smile as Will trudged out.

How was he going to explain? He could hardly say that he had travelled back in time from the twenty-first century with the aid of a mystical pendant, but he knew if he didn't do something, the princes would be doomed.

"I just know! You have to trust me. Maybe if they can't be moved, you could… double their guard or even move their lodgings to somewhere safer within the castle?"

Brackenbury sat down at his desk and looked at him.

"Becket, you expect me to double their guard on some childish whim? You haven't given me any reason why I should be concerned about their safety, and as for moving them, that's quite impossible."

Becket tried to think of something that would make him change his mind, but it was hopeless.

"I leave London today to join the King, who is on his way to York. I'm confident they will be safe until I return. Doctor Argentine is a good man and they are in very capable hands."

York! He was going to York. Brackenbury had to listen - to realise before it was too late the terrible danger the princes were in. He couldn't leave them.

"Please don't go!" Becket said.

"I'm sorry, but I have my responsibilities. I have to help plan the investiture of the King's son. He is to be crowned the Prince of Wales in York. It is likely to be a most splendid occasion," said Brackenbury, his eyes shining with pride. "If you have need of me urgently, send word to Sir John Grene. He is a man I trust. I have complete faith in him. Now hurry and catch young Will. The boys will soon be back from Morning Prayer and will require your services."

He had failed. Brackenbury hadn't listened to him. Why would he? He was just a boy. His best chance at getting home was leaving right now, but he couldn't just leave Richard and Edward without warning. He was torn, but as he reluctantly turned to leave, Brackenbury called after him.

"Becket, be sure to steer clear of the Duke. He will be furious when he finds that you are no longer his prisoner. I will do my best to manage him this time, but please, do not give him cause to lock you up again."

Becket didn't look up. He felt like screaming. He had no intention of being locked in the cold dungeon again. After he had warned the princes, he would find a way to follow Brackenbury to York. They would have to look after themselves. What more could he do?

Brackenbury gave Becket a last encouraging smile.

"Remember, if you really need my help, be sure to send word and I promise that I will do my utmost to return with all haste."

Becket once again found his way to the Garden Tower and was soon mounting the staircase that led to the young boys' apartments. He found them at breakfast with Will in nervous attendance, his skinny, shaking hands spilling the wine and clattering the plates as he tried to serve them. After Will and Becket had cleared away the dishes, Becket whispered to Richard,

"I need to talk to you. It's urgent. You are in the most terrible danger."

But before Richard could reply, three hot, sweating soldiers struggled into the room carrying a wooden crate. They dropped it to the floor with a crash, almost splintering the casket. Richard's eyes lit up.

"At last," he cried. "Good old gentle Brackenbury - always good to his word."

The soldiers pulled out three black iron cannonballs of differing sizes and placed them on the floor by the window. Richard went to examine them, bending over the battered balls, testing their weight.

"From the Ordnance Store. Brackenbury suggested we might like to examine some old shot. Thought it might relieve the boredom of being stuck in here all day. He's such thoughtful old fellow."

Edward looked up fingering his painful teeth.

"God's faith! These are so heavy," exclaimed Richard, grimacing as he tried to lift the largest ball. "I have no idea how the soldiers load these into the cannon."

As Richard grunted, Becket felt the weight of the others, managing to lift the smallest. Richard dismissed the soldiers and Edward came over from the table to the window ledge overlooking the gardens. He looked very ill. Becket looked around for the doctor.

"Where's Doctor Argentine?" he asked.

"He's been sent away," said Edward. "He was adamant he needed some more myrrh to help ease my pain, but the Duke overruled him. He said the good doctor's a spy and has been trying to poison me. Now I am left to cope with this pain alone. It's getting worse - I fear it will be the end of me."

"Does Brackenbury know?" Becket asked. "I'm sure he wouldn't allow it."

But Brackenbury had probably already left London to travel north to be with the King. It was all too convenient. All that stood between the princes and their enemies apart from a bunch of lazy soldiers were simple Black Will and himself. He grabbed Richard by the arm of his velvet tunic, leading him over to his brother by the window.

"You need to escape," Becket hissed. "Sir Robert has left London. I fear something dreadful is going to happen if you stay here."

"Do you not think that we know how perilous our position is?" Edward gasped. "Do you not think that we have spent every waking moment trying to think of a way out of this hateful place. We have been praying for salvation, yearning for a miracle! We live with the fear that at any moment the King could decide to be rid of us, just as he did with Uncle Rivers and dear Hastings. Who are you, a servant, to tell us that we need to escape? And why should we trust you, a mere page boy. What can be done when so many soldiers guard us day and night? Our position is hopeless. We will never get out of this place. The best we can hope for is that our uncle, the King forgets us."

Richard helped his brother to a chair.

"Don't be too hard on Becket, Edward," the younger boy said. "He's just trying to help, and our position is so fraught, what do we have to lose in trusting him? We can use all the help we can get."

Edward grimaced and said, "That's all very well, but Becket, how do you suggest we get out of here? If you hadn't already noticed, the Duke has his soldiers positioned all around this tower and they never let us out of their sight for a minute."

"What about your mother? She could help," asked Becket.

"Our mother is safely confined in Westminster Abbey," answered Richard. "I'm sure she would try to help us, but how are we to get word to her?"

Becket played with his hair. Edward looked like he might pass out with the pain. They helped him to the bedchamber. Becket thought of Bess. "My friend from the kitchen could get word to your mother," he suggested. "If I explained that you were in danger, I'm sure she would want to help. She certainly has no love for the Duke and his rat-like servant."

"Even if she managed to get into the Abbey, she would not be granted an audience," Richard said. "She is closely guarded by the Duke's soldiers."

Becket looked over at Will, who was shifting uneasily from foot to foot and trying not to be noticed. Becket asked him, "Will, maybe you…"

He got no further as the hapless boy interrupted him, "I would, but…but I have never been outside the castle walls and I'm sure I would lose my way. I would just mess things up."

Will hugged himself and rocked back and forth. Becket looked at Edward on the bed. The boy needed help.

"How are we to find a way out of here, Becket?" said Richard. "I don't trust the Duke of Buckingham or Lady Beaufort, and Bishop Morton is very clever. I fear we have some very powerful enemies. If only my father were still alive."

"I will go!" Becket suddenly exclaimed. "I will ask Bess. She is smart and I'm sure she'll help."

Richard looked doubtfully. Edward raised his head and said, "Thank you Becket. I'm sure you mean well and will try your best, but even if you manage to reach the sanctuary of the Abbey. How do you propose to gain access to our mother? And what can she do from there?"

Becket paced the room and Richard cried,

"I know a way! It's easy. I was in the Abbey with mother for just over a month and know the daily routine."

They listened as the younger boy explained,

"When people arrive at the Abbey seeking sanctuary, they confess their sins in return for the protection of the Church. The charter is now abused and the Abbey is now full of thieves and scoundrels. However, the sanctity of confession is still adhered to. There is a charitable priest, whose task it is to listen to the people's sins. He is a good man and was always kind to me and my sisters."

At this point, Richard pulled a golden locket and chain from over his head and placed it into Becket's hand.

"Show this to the priest and he will know immediately it belongs to me. This was my mother's locket, a gift to her from my father. She gave it to me when I left the Abbey. Our mother will grant you an audience on the strength of this locket. I am certain of it."

Becket placed the locket over his head and as it clanked against his own pendant, he couldn't help thinking how his own trinket was to blame for the mess he found himself in.

"I will go and find Bess," Becket said. "I'll be back before you know it."

He turned to Will, who now stood looking downcast at his dirty feet.

"Keep them safe until I return. If you think there is any danger, be sure to send word to Sir John Grene. Sir Robert told me he is a man who can be trusted."

Edward held out a feeble hand for Becket to take.

"I'm sorry, Becket. I didn't mean to sound ungrateful. I am thankful that you are here. What will become of us I know not, but at least you have given us some hope. Pray don't bother my mother with my illness. She will only worry, but I'm sure she will know how to act for the best. Please tell her about Lady Beaufort's visit and make sure she is aware of that the Duke keeps us closely guarded. Send her our love and stay safe. I wish you luck!"

Richard beamed at him, "I wish I was coming with you," he said. "What I wouldn't give to be part of such an adventure."

Becket had never been very good at goodbyes, so strode straight out of the room and toward the kitchens without another word.

Becket found Bess, as before, elbow deep in cold, discoloured water. She was scrubbing and peeling vegetables. She looked up at him with her big, blue eyes and seemed relieved to see him.

"Thank heaven, you are all right. I feared the worst when the soldiers took you away. I could not sleep for worrying."

"I'm fine," he replied, colouring a little," but I don't have much time and I really need your help."

He explained his fears for the safety of the princes now that Brackenbury had left London and his urgent need to get to Westminster Abbey to see their mother.

"It is too dangerous Becket. Are the princes in such jeopardy?" Bess countered with a worried frown. "Brackenbury would never have left them if he thought any harm would come to them. What can you do? Perhaps it would be best to wait until he comes back?"

"Trust me Bess. I understand the risk, but it's a matter of life and death."

"I don't think it's possible, Becket. The soldiers pay little heed to the workforce at the beginning and the end of each day, but if you try to leave at any other time they are likely to ask for an explanation. After your confrontation with the Duke, they will be looking out for you. There's no way you will be able to pass unnoticed."

"I could wear a disguise?"

Bess looked at him with a mocking smirk. "The best time to leave the castle is at the end of the day with the rest of the workforce. It is unlikely you would be noticed. But there is one big problem: you would need to be out of the city before the curfew bell tolls as nobody is allowed out after dark. The evening bell leaves you so little time - I fear you would not make it."

Bess adjusted her headscarf, poking at errant strands of thick hair.

"The only way out of the city is through one of the gates in the great surrounding wall. Ludgate would be your best chance. It's at the far end of the city, close to Westminster and provides the quickest route to the Abbey as it leads directly onto the Strand. But you must be through Ludgate before the gate closes - I really don't think it is possible. There won't be enough time. I'm sorry Becket - the risk is too great."

"Where exactly is Ludgate?"

"It's adjacent to the cathedral of St Paul," Bess answered. "If you can get through, the rest of the journey to Westminster is straightforward."

Becket recalled his trip to London the previous Christmas. The day he had been taken ice-skating at the Tower. It had poured all day, yet his dad had insisted that they cross Tower Bridge and walk down the south bank of the river toward the London Eye at Westminster. It had been a miserable, sodden walk and his dad had been keen to point out *HMS Belfast* (the old Second World War battleship moored on the Thames) and other curiosities, trying to save a pretty miserable day. Becket felt guilty – he had been so grumpy and sullen. What he wouldn't give to have that time again – to hold his mum's soft hands and to laugh at his dad's oversized raincoat.

"Becket? Becket, are you listening?"

The wet journey had taken less than an hour. He looked down at his trainers, remembering all his cross-country races. St Paul's Cathedral was closer to the Tower than the London Eye and even if he got a little lost; he should be able reach the gate in time.

"There is so little time between the two bells that I don't think you will make it," pleaded Bess.

"You haven't seen me run, Bess. These shoes are magic. They make me fly like the wind. The princes are depending on me. I have to give it a go!"

"Magic? You can fly like a bird? Are you truly a wizard, Becket?" asked Bess backing away.

"Just a figure of speech…"

Bess looked confused.

"I don't want you to go," Bess said suddenly stern.

"I have to and as soon as possible. With Brackenbury away the princes are defenceless," replied Becket.

Bess seemed like an older sister and although he knew she had his best interests at heart, he knew what he had to do.

Eventually she unhappily relented and began to scratch a map on the floor to show him the shortest route.

"Turn left into Tower Street and when you near St Paul's you will see Ludgate. Once through the gate you will be on the Strand and it's a simple journey from there, as long as you stay close to the river."

Becket nodded. He knew the London streets fairly well from all the tours his dad had made him endure. He would manage to find his way.

"Oh and Becket, you should wear these. The hat will hide your blonde hair."

Bess passed him a dirty looking cloak and a crumpled beret from a pile in the corner of the room.

"If you run into trouble, be sure to head for Walbrook Stream at the bottom of Watling Street. It's near the Great Bridge across the Thames and easy to find. Ask anyone there for 'Big Tom' and 'Little Tom' the tanners. That's my father and brother. I have told them about you and I'm sure they give you any help they can. Promise me you will be careful, Becket."

Becket squeezed Bess's wet hand and thanked her. He left the kitchen and jogged toward the exit gate. He wanted to get ahead of the crowd, but as he ran along the causeway, he noticed that apart from the soldiers lazing on the ramparts, the castle was deserted. Most of the people were still hard at work. He didn't want to take the risk of being stopped and questioned, so he turned around. He would have to be patient.

Becket noticed a flabby soldier guarding a gateway that lead down some worn steps and directly into the river. He remembered his dad explaining to him that the entrance from the Thames to the Tower was where all the political prisoners entered. His dad had called it 'Traitors' Gate.'

This soldier was dressed in a scarlet uniform, very unlike the dull brown outfits of all the regular soldiers. He was dozing and looked away timidly. He didn't look much of a guard.

CLANG! CLANG!

The tower bell signalled the end of the working day, Becket rushed toward the exit gates along with the mass of people pushing and shoving to get home, but the crowd was dense and so slow as people dawdled toward the exit. Becket was tightly squeezed in, and however hard he tried he couldn't make any headway and force his way to the front. A sense of nervous excitement tingled over him. It reminded him of the start of all the cross-country races back home. He was doing something positive and he was almost looking forward to the challenge.

Finally, Becket stepped out onto the wooden drawbridge and raced up Tower Hill. Turning left into Tower Street he tried to quicken his pace, but the narrow street was covered in a thick, slimy mud. It clung to his trainers. A mixture of animal dung and rotten food, it made fast progress impossible. His feet skidded and slipped and he almost fell over and lost his trainers in the deep sucking gunk. Becket slowed his pace. He couldn't afford a stupid accident.

A man wearing a clumpy pair of wooden shoes was raking the worst of the mud and muck into piles by the side of the street. He dodged a bucketful of filth that had been thrown from a first storey window. Looking up angrily the man shouted, "Don't be throwing your dung in the street! You know it's outlawed. I will report you to the alderman."

"Oh shut ye noise, muckraker," shrieked down a toothless crone. "You expect me to drag this filth to the river and get caught out after curfew? Just be getting on with your raking and leave honest folk to get about their business."

The man gave her a resigned look and continued piling up the mountains of putrid sludge.

Becket was an expert runner and in spite of the mud, was soon charging down the busy, meandering streets.

"Oyez, Oyez! The curfew bell is nigh," boomed a town crier, shaking a hand bell and causing Becket to jump in alarm.

Becket could hear his heart. He had to beat the clang of the curfew bell. Some small boys were sitting by the side of road and they leaped up as he dashed past, following him and crying out eagerly, "Give us a halfpenny?"

The little boys kept pace with him easily even though they were not wearing any shoes. Squelching after him, they persisted, "Slow down blondie-boy!"

Becket ignored them and kept running, causing the boys to finally fall behind and, resigned to a losing cause, firing some evil-smelling missiles in his direction as a farewell gift.

He ran faster until, in the distance, he saw a large wooden church that had to be St Paul's Cathedral. What a relief! Almost there! Then he heard a man shout from behind him, "Boy! Where are you running to in such a hurry? Slow down I want a word with you."

Becket slowed. A tall, bearded soldier was marching after him.

"Been stealing have we?" said the soldier. Becket ignored him and continued to trot steadily onward. "In the name of the King, I command you to halt! Stop right there!"

Becket started to sprint, losing his hat and the soldier in the process. He skipped past a small, flea-ridden, three-legged dog, hobbling miserably along the side of the road.

"Stop thief!" he heard the soldier shout.

He dashed onward until, at last, in the middle of the road ahead of him, was the formidable form of Ludgate. Similar to Micklegate in York, it was a large stone tower structure with an arched gateway and a portcullis that thankfully was still raised. The men guarding the gate didn't hear the soldier's cries, so Becket slowed to a walk and took a breath to calm himself. He looked up at the gate.

"Oh my goodness!"

There were several blue-brown bloated and rotting heads stuck on spikes. Crows were swooping down and pecking at their gruesome supper. Becket looked away and put his arm over his mouth to stop himself retching. Spitting on the road and taking in mouthfuls of air, he walked toward the open gateway. Nearly there - then Becket heard the muffled cry of the chasing soldier. If the guards heard him hollering, they would surely stop him and there would be no escape. He started to run as fast as he could.

"You boy! Halt!" bellowed one vigilant soldier as Becket bolted through the gate. Ducking underneath the guard's, Becket flew through the gate and without looking back, kept running and running, faster and faster, almost stumbling in his haste until he was sure he had to be safe. Panting with his hands on his knees, the curfew bell ringing in the distance, he looked back at the portcullis as it was locked fast for the night. Sweat stung his eyes. Becket couldn't believe his luck. Maybe he was going to actually pull this off! With renewed confidence, he began to walk toward Westminster.

The road was much wider than the streets within the city and he made steady progress. To his right, set back from the road, he noticed some large, well-built houses and to his left, the muddy-brown water of the Thames.

Keeping the river in sight, he trudged along in the fading light. Becket shivered - it was getting chilly. He needed to reach the Abbey before nightfall. The river straightened as more and more houses sprung out of the gloom. It couldn't be much further. A sprawling stone church, set back from the river suddenly dominated the horizon. It had to be the Abbey. Although not as impressive as the Tower or the Minster, it was a striking building with its tall Gothic towers looking down toward the Thames. He found himself in a busy lane full of shops shutting up for the night. Poorly built houses leaned over the centre of the lane, almost touching each other like a group of aged dancers stealing a kiss. It looked like a puff of wind could blow them over at any moment.

The gatehouse had a solitary, bored-looking guard at the gate. The soldier let him pass without a second glance. Becket found himself standing in a long corridor teeming with people: some slouching against the walls, some huddled together and sleeping on the rough stone floors, some playing at dice, others singing and drinking. Making his way through the crowd as fast as he could, Becket hurried on toward a church that sat beside the Abbey. He skirted around a fight that had broken out between two men playing at dice, and pushed away a tramp-like lady who tried to grab at his cloak. Finally entering the dark chilled building, Becket looked around. It seemed empty. A tired-looking clergyman walked toward him.

"Do you seek the sanctuary of the Abbey?" asked the churchman wearily. "You must confess your sins to be afforded the protection of the church?"

Becket nodded.

The priest led him to a dark alcove where two chairs were placed side by side. The priest indicated he should sit, and then sat himself. He started to whisper in a language that Becket guessed was Latin. The priest finally completed his chanting and looked up. This had to be the clergyman that Richard had mentioned.

"Father, I need your help."

The old man studied his fingernails.

"I must see Lady Elizabeth Woodville."

The priest looked up, his eyes narrowing.

"What business do you have with Her Ladyship? Are you another agent of the King sent here to trick her? She has been through so much already; why can't you people leave her in peace?"

Becket pulled out Richard's locket. The priest looked surprised.

"Who are you?" he demanded. "You are not Richard! You are an impostor! What do you want from me? That belongs to Prince Richard. How did you come by it?"

"I am Richard's friend. He gave me his locket - he knew you would recognise it. I am page to the royal princes at the Tower. They are in great danger. I must see their mother, the Lady Elizabeth, before it's too late."

"Richard would never have let it out of his sight. Has something happened to him?"

"I need to see her right away..." Becket was frantic. He had come so far, the priest had to help him.

"I'm not sure who you are, but I'm sure Her Ladyship will want to hear how you came by the locket." The priest levered himself to his feet, opened the small door and led Becket out by his arm. "We cannot talk here. There are spies everywhere," grumbled the old clergyman and holding out his hand continued, "Give me the locket. I will take it to Her Ladyship. She trusts nobody, but perhaps she will grant you an audience." Snatching the trinket he rushed off.

Becket was in the great hall of the Abbey. He sat down on a stone bench alongside a tomb. He was so thirsty. Looking down at his mud-splattered trainers, he thought back to his mad dash through the city. He had actually enjoyed it. Running was such a large part of his life. Would he ever get home to race again? The alternatives didn't bear thinking about and pulling his cloak tightly around him, he rested his head on the cold stone.

CHAPTER 8
LADY ELIZABETH WOODVILLE

Becket lay in the darkness. The flickering candles barely lit up the vast room - he felt uneasy. Then he heard a voice; hardly a whisper, followed by the tapping of footsteps coming closer. He lay stock-still. Two men were arguing and as they came closer he could hear one of them,

"The princes!"

Then something he couldn't hear followed by,

"Buckingham!"

As the footsteps drew nearer Becket began to hear more fragments of the conversation.

"They are more than an inconvenience. They block Henry's path to the throne. Our plans will come to nothing unless they are removed. Luckily the whole of London expects the King to find a way to be rid of them. We will never have a better opportunity and if it is handled correctly the blame will fall on the King."

"But what about Buckingham?"

"Don't worry about him. He's a vain fool. He would do anything to increase his power. He covets the throne himself. I have him on a tight leash. That pompous peacock may actually come in very useful in the future."

Becket lay still, holding his breath. He had heard the voices somewhere before. The first man sounded older than the other and to be leading the conversation.

"*And Lady Beaufort?*" asked the younger man.

"*She is well aware of what's at stake and is impatient that these obstacles are removed as quickly as possible.*"

The prince's lives were in imminent danger. But who were these men? They were now so close that he could hear one of them rubbing his hands together. He had to find a better hiding place. Slipping onto the floor, he crawled toward a sarcophagus and squeezed behind it.

"*My mistress…the King of France…will finance the invasion… Lord Stanley will muster an army, but not until the boys are disposed of.*"

The voices became fainter and as Becket tried shifting his weight, one of the large stone slabs beneath him gave way with a horrible grinding noise and he tumbled down into darkness.

He hit the stone floor with a clump. His back burned with pain. Then there were running footsteps and a voice,

"*What was that noise?*"

"*I don't know, but it sounded like a stone falling. Maybe somebody has been spying on us. I wonder how much they heard,*" replied the other uncertainly.

"*Do you think it was one of the King's men?*"

"*Possibly or Lady Woodville's. There are spies everywhere.*"

Becket curled into a ball as he heard the men above, praying he wouldn't be discovered. He looked around him. He seemed to be in a small recess, beneath the ancient tomb. Then the voices suddenly ceased. They must have given up. Becket brushed some cobwebs from his face and almost screamed as he felt something crawl over his hand. Squirming in the darkness, he remembered where he had heard the voices before. Back in the Tower: the men with Lady Beaufort, Bishop Morton and the man called Bray - he was certain of it! He had to get back to the Tower. He had to warn the princes before something terrible happened. But without their mother's help it would be impossible.

The whole chamber suddenly seemed brighter, and looking down Becket saw that the pendant was throwing out a pale purple light. Pulling it toward him for a closer look, he yelped and hastily withdrew his hand. The pendant was scorching. Was it trying to warn him, to tell him something or was it about to propel him into another time and place? Looking around, Becket was petrified he was going to spy a skeleton or a skull, but the chamber was empty. He noticed a very faint drawing scratched on the wall. Brushing away some cobwebs, it looked like two knights astride a single horse. Who could have been doodling down in this hellhole? It gave him the creeps. The light began to fade as the pendant once more came becalmed. Becket looked back to the wall, but the drawing had disappeared into the murk. Something crawled across the back of his neck – he couldn't stand it any longer. Scrambling out of the recess, slapping at his back, he peered into the shadows of the Abbey. The cathedral was deserted – the men had gone.

He was brushing away the last of the cobwebs and dust from his clothes, when the churchman came shambling toward him.

"Good morning young man. I trust you are well rested and ready to see her Ladyship?"

Becket thought it best not to mention the episode with Bishop Morton and Bray. He couldn't trust anyone, not even the priest, and who was likely to believe his story anyway? It would be a young boy's word against those of two powerful and influential men. He would keep the whole thing a secret until he could get back to the Tower and warn the princes.

"Come with me," ordered the old priest. "Her Ladyship is waiting. I fear her patience is running rather thin as she has several important people seeking an audience with her this morning."

Becket followed him along an arched corridor that skirted a courtyard within the Abbey. The rushes that lined the floor rustled under their feet as the man scurried along, nodding to several monks on the way. After passing through a garden, they arrived at an impressive house that sat at the perimeter of the Abbey. Becket was ushered through the door and into a room with high ceilings and colourful tapestries. The floor was covered in glazed green and red diamond-shaped tiles set in an ornate pattern. It almost seemed a shame to stand on such marvellous craftwork. At the end of the room, on the edge of an intricately carved chair, sat a beautiful woman, whom Becket guessed to be the prince's mother, Lady Elizabeth Woodville.

Although no longer Queen of England, she had the bearing of a true royal. The petite, elegantly dressed lady had a thin, pale and incredibly beautiful face. Her light brown hair was scraped back and hidden in a soft gold bonnet that balanced precariously on the back of her head. She wore a dark purple velvet dress and a gold-trimmed cloak of the same colour that sat neatly on her bare flawless white shoulders. Her bloodshot eyes looked very weary, but she seemed in complete control of herself and her surroundings. A small lapdog scampered around her feet looking hopefully for treats.

She dismissed the priest and beckoned Becket toward her. To her side sat seven young girls, equally glamorously attired: presumably her daughters and therefore the prince's sisters. The eldest appeared to be in her late teens and a replica of her mother. She had the same self-assured expression on her equally striking face and the same light brown hair and blue eyes. One of the other daughters, who seemed just a little older than Becket and unfortunately bearing a striking resemblance to the lap dog, couldn't stifle a girlish giggle as he stumbled on the tiled floor whilst attempting an unpractised bow in his baggy cloak.

"Be quiet Cecily! Remember who you are. I will not have you acting like a common washer girl," admonished her mother.

The young girl buried her face in her handkerchief.

"I do not have time for niceties young man. Tell me who you are and how you came to be in possession of this locket?"

Before Becket could reply, she dismissed her younger daughters, leaving only the eldest two sitting either side of her. Lady Elizabeth stared at Becket, "Explain yourself!"

Becket told her his story: how he had been appointed as a page to the princes and about his fears for their safety. He told her of Lady Margaret Beaufort's visit and the Duke sending the doctor away, but thought it wise not to mention his suspicions of Bishop Morton and Bray before he had warned the two boys. Lady Elizabeth listened, stopping him occasionally to question him. When he had finished she stood up, placing her hands together in front of her pale pink lips as if in prayer. He waited for her to speak. The silence seemed to last forever. Cecily seemed more interested in his jeans and trainers than his story and with another snigger, whispered something into her elder sister's ear. Lady Elizabeth frowned at her daughters and finally spoke.

"You can leave us ladies. Go see to your sisters." Turning to Becket she continued, "Young man, your story has the ring of truth. Lady Beaufort pursues the claim of her son, Henry, relentlessly, whilst he hides overseas. She is a dangerous lady. Buckingham is just the King's pawn and can be managed, but Lady Beaufort is an entirely different proposition."

Lady Elizabeth rose and paced up and down.

"Your timing is most expeditious. I have an audience with Sir James Tyrell shortly. He is a clever and honourable man that I can trust. I am sure he will know what can be done."

She walked to the door and shouted to an attendant to take Becket to the kitchens to ensure that he was given food and drink. She would see him again after her interview with Tyrell.

Becket wolfed down his breakfast He was starving. If only he could get back to York. Pulling out his pendant, he studied it closely. It held the key to the mystery. He had to find the way to harness its power. It was the only chance he had of getting back home. Becket frantically poked and prodded the dark stone, tracing his fingers lightly over the strange shape at its centre. It seemed to be mocking him. Maybe the Quire Screen was some kind of portal – a gate in time. But how was he going to get back there? There were no trains or cars. He might as well be on the moon. Why had it come to life in the small crypt? Was it trying to give him a clue? Had he been sent back in time for a reason - to save the princes? His mind was a muddle of unanswered questions, but it was futile - the pendant had a life of its own and he let the maddening thing flop back onto his chest. He didn't know how he was going to get home, but of one thing he was certain: he mustn't lose the magic charm.

The priest reappeared and said, "Come on young man, Her Ladyship wants to see you again. Follow me."

Becket was again ushered into the former queen's presence. This time she was alone.

She gestured for him to sit down on a small chair beside her.

"I will be brief," she said. "I have consulted with Sir James and he has proposed the following plan. He will have a boat ready at Billingsgate Quay to sail for Flanders two days hence. The boat can wait there for two further days, but no longer. We do not want to arouse suspicion. The Duke has all the jetties and ports watched and his agents are posted all over the city. We cannot give him an excuse to lock my poor boys in the depths of the Tower. We have one chance and if we fail, I fear they will never see the light of day again."

She spoke without emotion and pulled out a small leather pouch and dropped the locket into his hands.

"Take the locket back to Richard. When they reach the boat, they must show it to the master. Do you understand, Becket? I have no idea how you will manage to help my sons escape, but if you do the boat will be waiting to carry them over the seas to safety."

Tears were in her eyes.

"I wish you luck. You are indeed a courageous young man. I am glad my sons have found such a true and trusted servant."

The door burst open and ignoring the protestations of the priest, Lady Margaret Beaufort strode into the room. Becket groaned. She approached Lady Elizabeth, anger blazing in her fierce, jet-black eyes. Becket wished he could melt into the tiled floor. He was scared stiff. The room suddenly seemed colder, and his body was tense as Beaufort faced the former queen in her ludicrous peaked hat and nun-like dress.

"Lady Elizabeth, I have been kept waiting too long."

Lady Elizabeth showed no sign of fear, as she sat still, her hands clasped on her lap.

"I await your answer," Lady Beaufort continued. "Have you reached a decision? Will your daughter Elizabeth agree to be betrothed to my son, Henry?"

Bishop Morton and Bray had followed Lady Beaufort into the room and were stood a few paces behind her.

Becket hoped the two men wouldn't notice him.

"Good morning Lady Beaufort. It's so nice to see you again - and so soon," replied Lady Elizabeth icily. "I have not changed my mind. I still do not see your son as a match for my eldest daughter, Elizabeth. If I should change my mind, I will be sure to let you know."

Lady Beaufort scowled, tapping her foot impatiently.

"Don't play games with me Lady Woodville. Your sons are declared illegitimate. The King doesn't have the support of the people, as they believe he has no right to the throne. The only chance your family has of regaining any influence or power is by joining forces with me. An agreed betrothal between your daughter and my son, Henry, will unite the Houses of York and Lancaster and the country will be sure to rally to our cause."

"My son Edward is the true and rightful King of England. Whilst he draws breath I do not see how your son has any claim to the throne," replied Lady Elizabeth.

Bishop Morton walked forward, rubbing his hands together, but Lady Beaufort spoke, "These are confused and trouble times, Lady Woodville, and life is a precarious thing. Your sons are young and vulnerable position and I would suggest that you choose your friends wisely."

"Is that a threat Lady Beaufort?"

"I do not issue threats, Lady Woodville. Think carefully on what I have said. Please make haste with your decision. Time is running out for you and those that you love."

With this last statement, Lady Beaufort turned to leave when she saw Becket standing behind Lady Woodville.

"Who is this boy? What's that he's wears around his neck?"

She peered at his pendant.

"Where did you get this?"

Becket's face coloured as he pulled the cloak tightly around him in an attempt to hide his pendant.

"I asked you a question boy. I demand to know where you got that valuable trinket."

Becket wanted to run from the room and get as far away as possible from the wicked old lady.

"He is a trusted servant of my family and has my protection," answered Lady Elizabeth.

Bray stepped forward and whispered something into the old lady's ear.

"That is quite correct Bray. How clever of you to remember. He was one of the boys attending the princes the last time we visited the Tower."

She made a grab for the pendant, but Becket stepped back.

"That pendant belongs to me. He must have stolen it. Arrest this boy!" she screamed.

"Don't be so ridiculous Lady Beaufort. Our interview is at an end, please stop browbeating my servant. I know the jewel to be his property. You are mistaken I bid you a good day."

Lady Beaufort glared at Becket. "I will reclaim which is rightly mine. You haven't heard the last of this."

She thundered out of the room with the Bishop and Bray hurrying after her

Lady Woodville seemed unflustered. "I wish you good luck young Becket. I am afraid Lady Beaufort will not be denied and I cannot stall for much longer. My sons' lives depend on you. Please do not fail them."

As Becket left the room, he looked back and saw the former queen with her tiny dog on her lap, sobbing into the folds of its fur.

Becket left the Abbey and went down towards the river. Ambling along, he thought of the Lady Elizabeth and her tears. His own mother would be the same. What would his aunt be thinking? Becket looked up and saw two ruffians standing in front of him, barring his path. They smirked and pinned his arms behind him, dragging him to into a nearby courtyard and throwing him to the ground. Lady Beaufort sneered down at him.

"Who are you?" she demanded.

Bray dismissed the men. "Answer Her Ladyship!"

"Where did you get the Abraxus stone?" she barked, tapping her feet in impatience.

"It's a present - from my aunt."

"Your aunt?" repeated Lady Beaufort. "Fie! Give it to me."

What was he to do? To give up the pendant would be a disaster. It was his only way home.

"Take it Bray!" Lady Beaufort ordered.

There was nowhere to run. He was penned in with his back to the wall.

Bray moved towards him. The pendant began to throb violently, beaming out a purple ray of light.

Bray made a grab for it but screamed in pain and sharply pulled his hand away. His hand was burned. Becket could smell smouldering flesh as the pendant vibrated wildly and shone brighter than ever. Bray reached out for leather string to rip it from his neck, but was flung against the courtyard wall by some invisible force, crashing into a bush.

"You fool, Bray!" shrieked the old lady. "I will have it, even if I have to take it myself."

The pendant was now a frenzy of light. As Lady Beaufort lunged at Becket she was also propelled across the courtyard, landing next to Bray, where she lay moaning and rubbing her head.

This was his chance. Becket hurdled over them and raced out into the street.

Suddenly, the two thugs were behind him. Becket broke into a sprint, weaving his way through the ever-growing crowd like a demented wasp. But the men were getting nearer and nearer. Becket looked behind anxiously and didn't see a clapped-out cart in front of him. He crashed into it, falling to the floor. The men lifted him to his feet. Becket winced in pain.

Within seconds Bray had joined them. "Take this boy to Coldharbour." Bray's singed hand was wrapped in a linen cloth. "Make sure he's secure. Her Ladyship will join you shortly. She has some business at Westminster to attend to then she will want to deal with this little pest herself."

Bray walked back toward the Abbey.

One of the men sniggered and twisted Becket's arm. "Coldharbour, that'll be the end of you, boy. Once you're in that cellar, you ain't comin' out."

Becket cried out in pain. Coldharbour – what or where was that?

He was dragged down the road toward the city.

The other man spoke, "I don't like it. There's something not right with that place. It's possessed by the devil."

"Possessed by Her Ladyship more like," replied the other.

Becket was scared. He didn't like the sound of Coldharbour. If they took his pendant, he was lost. The boys would be beyond help and more importantly his path home would be gone.

"Sometimes Her Ladyship goes in and don't come out for months. It ain't natural..." one of the men said.

"Don't be daft. Must be a secret entrance thereabouts. Only explanation," interrupted the other man.

"That or the devil's magic."

They were now at Ludgate. A crowd of people were forming a rowdy queue, flanked by soldiers looking on. The two men pushed their way toward the front. What was he going to do? He had to think of something and quickly. Then he saw his chance. In front of him, a giant of a man carrying two large baskets of cabbages on his shoulders was shuffling toward the gate. Becket jerked away from the men and leapt up and pulled down hard on one of the baskets, causing the cabbages to spill all over the ground. Then, ducking under the wheels of a nearby cart, he began to crawl along. The men tried to get at him, but were engulfed in the melee as people jostled for the bounty.

The man with the baskets let out a loud roar, grabbing one of the men by the waist and lifting him off the ground. The man shrieked and some of the soldiers tried to intervene. Becket saw his chance. Darting out from beneath the cart, he rushed through the gateway and raced down the first side street, half-expecting to be grasped from behind at any moment. He ran as fast as he could, through the twisting lanes, racing between houses. He hurdled a wide, stout pig that stood lazily in the middle of the street, and skidded to halt. There was a concealed path leading off to the left and Becket charged down it and collapsed behind an oversized wooden barrel, gasping for breath. He put his fist in his mouth to calm his heavy breathing and listened. All he could hear were horses' hooves and shopkeepers shouting.

Becket waited for a few minutes more, then tentatively ventured back to the lane.

There was no sign of the men. Apart from the odd beggar, nobody took any notice of him. A dirty dwarf of a man approached him, asking a price for his teeth. Becket pushed him away and tying his hoodie around his waste, hurried on. It was so hot and he was thirsty. What now? The streets all looked the same. How was going to get back to the Tower? Then he remembered Bess's last words to him.

"If you need help be sure to seek out my father and brother at Walbrook Stream."

She said that they lived near London Bridge. That shouldn't be difficult to find and once there he would be able to find her family. Hopefully they would let him stay the night and then he could try and get back into the Tower along with Bess in the morning. He approached a man, smoking a clay pipe, sitting on a stool at the side of the road and asked him for directions. The bewildered man looked at him as if he were a madman, but pointed to a street on Becket's right. Becket walked cautiously onward, keeping a watchful eye for any sign of the men. At least he had lost them for now.

Becket wrinkled his nose. He could smell the pungent waft of the river. The medieval people used the poor old Thames as a handy rubbish dump and public sewer and it smelled dreadful. As he came to the end of a steeply banking lane, he finally saw the river stretched out in front of him.

The Thames was a mess of sails with boats and barges fighting for space on the fast-flowing water. Then Becket saw the bridge. It was covered from end to end with houses and all manner of shops, all perched hazardously like a giant 'Jenga' game on either side of a central thoroughfare that was full of horses, carts and people creating a medieval traffic jam. At each end was a drawbridge, one of which was now being raised to allow a tall ship to sail through.

The bridge looked like it may collapse and sink into the river at any moment. Looking up, Becket immediately closed his eyes. Rusted spikes holding aloft withered heads were strewn across the top of the bridge. He turned away in disgust, suddenly hating the sick people of medieval England and their cruelty. Becket walked away from the river. He had to find Walbrook Stream and there, hopefully the safety of Bess's family home.

Walking northward, he obtained further directions from a butcher and turned into a waterlogged lane. Dodging the muddy puddles as best he could, he came upon a slow-moving stream that flowed down to the Thames. The banks were filled with people washing and cleaning pots, pans, blankets and sheets. He approached a man wearing an apron, washing what appeared to be an animal hide, and asked him if he knew the whereabouts of "Big and Little Tom". The man growled at him suspiciously and pointed upstream. After a few minutes, Becket came across a young man wearing a similar apron, also washing hides in the stream. He was very muscular and had a shock of thick chestnut hair that drooped over his freckled face. The likeness was unmistakeable. This had to be Bess's brother.

He approached him and politely enquired, "Excuse me, but are you Tom? Bess's brother, Tom?"

The young man continued washing the hides. "Who wants to know?"

"My name is Becket. I'm a friend of your sister, Bess. She said if I was in need of help to seek you out."

The young man looked up, and lifting the sodden hide onto his shoulders, beckoned for him to follow.

Becket was led through a yard filled with steaming stinking barrels. The stench stabbed at the back of his throat and he threw his arm over his nose and mouth.

"Never smelled boiling hides before eh? It's only animal pee," Little Tom snorted and pointing to one of the evil-smelling barrels.

"Does a fine job of removing the animal hair, ready for the scraping and the tanning."

Bess's brother stirred the contents of the barrel with a wooden stick. Becket couldn't take it anymore and lurched off to the side of the yard and vomited. He felt ashamed, but hastily wiped his mouth and looked up to see, sitting on a stool outside a small, wooden-framed shack, a lean middle-aged man scraping an animal hide with a small, blunt knife. His clouded, drawn face stared into the distance as his expert hands scraped away at the hide.

"Father, this is that boy that Bess mentioned," said Bess's brother. "We should have no part of this and send him on his way. It is bound to end badly for all of us. It's none of our business."

The old man waved his son away.

"Go and clean the last of the hides, Tom. The day is nearly done and Bess will be home soon to see to the supper."

He got up from his stool and gestured for Becket to follow him into the shack. The solitary room was dimly lit and warm. The floor was covered with straw and a fire was smouldering on a stone hearth. The old man pointed to one of the two wooden crates that sat in the middle of the room next to a wonky, trestle table and asked him to sit down. The room was sparse: mud-caked walls, a large oak chest and three dirty, straw-filled mattresses piled on top of one another in the far corner. Bess's father poured him some beer.

"You are welcome in our home young man. Bess tells me you have been a good friend to her. For that I thank you and offer you the meagre hospitality my home provides. She will be back shortly as it will soon be curfew. You had best spend the night here unless you want to be locked up by the soldiers."

Bess's father then walked back out into the yard to help his son close down for the day.

The combination of the intoxicating beer, the choking smoke and the stifling heat of the fire made Becket feel sleepy. He soon began to doze and his head lolled from side to side as he desperately tried to stay awake. He was keen to see Bess and tell her about his adventures and his meeting with Lady Woodville and her daughters. He was also impatient to find out the news of the two boys. It was strange that for once he wasn't thinking of home. He needed to help the princes. Everything else could wait.

CHAPTER 9

ESCAPE

Bess's freckled face looked down at Becket. She offered him a bowl of steaming soup.

"Potage, Becket?" Bess asked.

Becket thought it an odd choice for breakfast, but he was starving, so gratefully accepted.

"Eat it while it's hot as we need to be on our way soon."

He struggled into a sitting position, rubbing his tired eyes, still half-asleep. Bess reminded him of his mum, clucking and scolding him first thing before school. He looked at her as she busied herself tidying away the breakfast things – he was pleased to see her again.

"Father and Tom have already gone to work. We thought it was best to let you sleep."

Becket gulped down the thick, salty vegetable soup. He wanted to ask Bess about the princes and tell her about his adventures at the Abbey, but as he started to talk, she cut him short.

"There's a barrel of water in the yard. You can wash there, but hurry. If we are late it will only draw the attention of the soldiers."

Having dipped his head into the freezing cold water and dusted down his soiled clothes, Becket was ready. Bess led him through the streets in silence. The sun was just starting to poke its head above the cluster of houses when she spoke.

"So, did you manage to see Lady Woodville?" she asked.

"Yes I did."

"I hear she is very attractive for a woman of her age and her daughters are much admired," continued Bess, her eyes fixed on the road ahead.

"Yes, she is a very beautiful and I met two of her daughters, Elizabeth and Cecily."

Bess quickened her pace and Becket almost had to jog as he laboured along behind her.

"Well, I suppose with the aid of fine dresses and never having to work, it's a little easier to look beautiful!"

The Tower loomed in front of them and Becket once again found himself amongst the noisy crowd trudging into the famous castle.

A soldier shouted down from the ramparts,

"Good morning Bess. The day is as almost as lovely as you!"

Bess ignored him and continued slowly onward. Another soldier ushering the crowd through the gate grinned at Bess,

"A sight for sore eyes. Beauteous 'Red Bess'. Always a joyous way to start the day."

Bess tightened her headscarf.

Becket couldn't help teasing Bess, "Nice to be so popular!"

"This hair is a curse. I can never pass unnoticed and the soldiers never miss an opportunity to pester and taunt me."

"Well, I think your hair is fabulous. It isn't a curse at all. You should be very proud of it."

She coloured and gave him a grateful smile. "My father often says I am my mother's double."

They had arrived in the main square of the castle, and as Bess rushed off toward the kitchen Becket called after her.

"I will come and see you later and tell you about my adventures."

Without turning, she waved him a hasty farewell and Becket once more headed toward the state apartments. He was keen to see the two princes and hatch an escape plan.

He bumped into Will, sitting on his perch at the window with his head resting on his bony, grubby hands.

The boy jumped up as soon he saw him and said, "Becket, I am so… so pleased that you are back. I tried so hard to get a message to Sir John, but…that man Forest. He grabbed the note and tore it up."

"What's wrong Will?" asked Becket.

Will pushed Becket to the staircase. Walking into the apartments, he saw Richard, sitting at the table writing a note.

"Thank the Lord you made it back. Did you manage to see my mother?" asked Richard.

"Where's Edward?" Becket asked.

"Edward is in bed," Richard answered. "I think he may be dying."

"Dying? Is it his teeth?" asked Becket.

"No, this time he's complaining of severe cramping and he has a terrible fever."

Becket asked why they hadn't summoned Doctor Argentine. Richard looked crestfallen. They had tried, but the Duke had refused. Instead he had sent one of his own physicians, who had given Edward a draught to ease the pain.

Becket didn't like the sound of that.

"When did the pains start?"

"After supper on the day you left us."

"Do you still have the medicine the physician gave him?"

"No. He makes sure Edward swallows it before he leaves, but it seems to make him worse. I'm really worried Becket."

The young prince looked close to tears.

Becket sat him down and said, "Now listen to me and don't panic. It's going to be all right, but I think your brother may be being poisoned. He mustn't take any more of the medicine and we must try and get word to Brackenbury as soon as possible."

"I fear Edward won't last that long," choked a tearful Richard.

A thought flashed through Becket's mind.

He remembered his aunt's potions and remedies. What had she told him about poison? She had said that dandelions had helped her arthritis, but what was it she said would help if you swallowed something poisonous? Mulberry leaves mixed with vinegar. He shouted at Will to hurry to the kitchen, find Bess and ask her if she could track down the ingredients.

"Hurry, Will," he shouted. "Tell Bess it's a matter of life and death!"

Becket followed Richard into the bedroom where he saw Edward, deathly pale, laying on the soft bed.

"Becket, you are back," Edward croaked.

"I have sent for a potion I hope will help you. You must be strong. I have seen your mother and she has arranged for a boat that will take you both to the safety. Don't worry, we will make you better and then we can come up with a plan to get you both out of this place and away from danger."

Edward looked at Becket. "I am afraid I am destined to never leave this place. Dear old Rivers, I miss him so. I shall make peace with God…"

Edward suddenly leaned forward and grabbed Becket by the arm tightly and whispered fervently, "But Becket, you must help Richard. He is young and has such a life ahead of him."

"Enough of this talk," Richard broke-in cheerfully. "I am not sure what I would do without your constant whining about your infernal teeth. A little ague is all that ails you and clever Becket will soon sort that out. You are going to be fine."

Edward looked earnestly into his brother's face and said, "Richard, dear brother, swear to me that if you manage to escape this hateful place you will never try and regain the throne. Promise me you will relinquish your claim. Kingship has been the death of so many of our family - our grandfather, uncles, cousins and even our poor father. Power corrupts, sweet brother. You must lead a peaceful life. Marry, have children who will never know what it is to have the shadow of the throne looming over them."

Edward collapsed back onto the pillow, his laboured breathing echoing around the chamber. Becket left the room and sat down at the table with Richard and recounted the events of his trip to Westminster Abbey. He told him about meeting the old priest, Lady Woodville and his two sisters, and overhearing Bray and Bishop Morton's evil plotting.

"Heavens!" exclaimed Richard. "I knew Lady Beaufort was passionate about her son's claim to the throne, but I didn't think the Bishop would stoop this low. Bray is a clever man. He always seems to end up on the winning side."

Their conversation was interrupted by the noise of soldiers shouting and whistling below. They both looked up as the door opened and Bess strode into the room followed by Will. Her face was red and she looked furious. She carried a basket on her arm, which she banged down on the table, before curtseying respectfully to the young prince.

"I brought the things that you asked for, Becket. It wasn't easy to escape from the kitchen. Luckily the soldiers were too busy teasing me to notice what was in the basket."

Thanking her, Becket emptied the contents onto the table and quickly set to work with a handy ladle, crushing the leaves into a pulp and mixing them into a bowl with the vinegar. When he had finished, he was left with an unctuous green mixture that actually didn't smell too bad.

Bess lifted Edward's head gently and spooned some of the mixture into his mouth. He spluttered and coughed and most of the slimy mixture ran down his chin leaving a green stain on the white sheets. Bess gently persisted until she had emptied almost half of the bowl. Edward lay back on the bed for a minute and then leaning over, vomited all over the floor. Richard and Bess looked concerned, but Becket assured them that he thought it a good thing, as it was purging Edward's body of the potent poison.

"We will need plenty more I'm afraid Bess, as every time he is given a draught, we will need to repeat the dose. He needs to rid his system of the poison before it can take effect."

Will helped Bess clear up the messy floor while Becket sat at the table, brooding with his eyes half-closed.

He suddenly looked up and asked Bess, "Would it be possible to smuggle a spare set of your clothes into these apartments? Maybe you could hide them under your dress?"

Bess looked at him as if he was crazy.

"A spare set of clothes? I suppose so, but what would you need them for?"

"I have an idea," he replied.

Bess put on her shawl. "I have to go or I shall be missed. I will be back tomorrow with the clothes and more mulberry and vinegar."

Edward's breathing seemed more regular and the fever seemed to have abated. Richard thanked Becket for his help.

"You are clever indeed, Becket. You seem so wise and know so many things. Did you learn such things in your country? Is life very different there?"

"My country," answered Becket, "is not so very different. The sun still comes up in the morning, but we have things you could hardly dream of. We have metal carriages that need no beasts to draw them. At the push of a pedal they can travel faster than the sturdiest of warhorses. We have houses that fly in the sky quicker than the speediest of birds, carrying people across the seas to foreign lands."

Richard looked incredulous.

"Flying machines?"

"We have hospitals where all the sick people are cared for and cured with all sorts of marvellous medicines."

Richard looked at him doubtfully. "Is this true? Do you really have such things in your land? I wish I could go there. It would be truly wonderful to be able to fly like a bird and travel as fast as the wind."

Becket eyes watered, feeling sorry for himself. The modern world with all its comforts seemed so far away. He wondered if he would ever travel in a car, watch television or just have a hot bath again.

"We need to get you out of here. Do you think Edward will go with you?"

"I don't think so. He is weak. The death of our father and Rivers has hit him very hard. The disease in his teeth has sapped his strength. I fear that without the good doctor's help, he will never recover."

Their conversation was interrupted by a bang on the door. Two soldiers marched into the room followed by a small bald man in a long black gown carrying a brass jug.

"I have come on the instruction of His Grace, the Duke of Buckingham, to administer Prince Edward's medicine," he said.

"He is sleeping, doctor," answered Richard.

"Then I shall have to wait. His Grace was very clear that I should not leave before Prince Edward had taken the full draught. I am told that he must be fit enough to leave these apartments by dusk tomorrow."

"Leave these apartments?" exclaimed Richard. "On whose orders?"

"His Grace has decided that it would be safer and more convenient for you both to move into rooms adjacent to the chapel in the White Tower. It will save your brother the daily journey and His Grace is concerned that there may be a foreign spy at large who means you harm."

Becket clenched his fists. He was more concerned by the scheming Bray and Morton than the pompous Duke, but he was obviously up to something.

Edward woke up and cried out for his brother. Becket followed Richard and the doctor into the bedroom. The younger boy helped his brother drink a small cup of beer, as the doctor poured out a small vial of dark liquid into a goblet. Richard turned and was about to berate the man when Becket caught his eye. He glanced over at the remaining mulberry and vinegar and put his fingers to his lips to warn Richard to stay silent. The doctor administered the draft, pouring it slowly down Edward's throat until the unfortunate boy started to cough uncontrollably. Only then did the physician leave, flanked by the soldiers, satisfied that he had completed his task.

Becket dashed over to the half empty bowl of mulberry and vinegar and rushing to Edward's side, he spooned the remaining mixture into the boy's mouth. The prince gulped it down and vomited. Richard mopped Edward's sweat glistened forehead, gripping his hand as he drifted off to sleep.

Richard left for evening prayers, leaving Becket alone with Edward. Looking around the apartment, Becket noticed his satchel sitting in the corner. Walking over and opening it, he pulled out his Swiss Army penknife. It was an ingenious invention. The small red knife had numerous tools hidden within its shiny handle. There was a corkscrew, a pair of scissors, a nail file, some tweezers, a screwdriver and other useful attachments. It was a little rusty, but he took it everywhere with him. He looked out of the window at the gardens below and started to scrape at the stone with his knife. The stone crumbled easily and he had soon made a smooth round hole. He scratched his initials and his date of birth and stood back to admire his handiwork.

The following morning the bell tolled to signal another day. Workers streamed into the castle. Becket looked up from his place by the window as a harassed looking Bess entered the room.

"Those soldiers are just too annoying and I am so very hot," said a perspiring Bess, as she pulled her sackcloth dress over her head, revealing an almost identical one underneath. He took the discarded dress and hooded cloak and hid them under the bed.

"I must go to work now, Becket. I am already late," said Bess as she placed another basket of mulberry leaves and a jug of vinegar on the table.

"Thank you, Bess. Our patient is a little better. I think the potion seems to be working. Would it be possible for you to sneak back just before the evening bell?" asked Becket.

"I suppose so. The head cook favours me, so I should be able to manage it," Bess replied.

Richard slammed the door behind him and looking livid, threw his leather prayer book across the room almost knocking the jug of vinegar off the table.

"What's wrong?" asked Becket, halting his scratching of the wall and putting his knife away.

"The Duke of Buckingham, Becket. He tried to stop me from coming back here. He has set up a small bedchamber close to the chapel and refused to let me return. Luckily, he was distracted when that man Bray arrived and I ordered the soldiers to bring me back."

"Bray is here? Was Morton with him?"

"No, but I overheard them talking. The bishop has gone to the Duke's castle in Brecon. What are we going to do, Becket? If they get us into the White Tower we will never escape."

"I have a plan, but we need to stall them for as long as possible. Do you know where Billingsgate Quay is Richard?"

"Yes of course. I was often ferried up and down the river in the royal barge when my father was alive."

"And you have your locket?"

"Of course," replied Richard pulling the locket out from under his tunic.

"OK. Follow me into the bedroom and I will tell you the plan. It's not perfect, but with a little bit of luck, you never know!"

Bess arrived back as she had promised, but looked flustered.

Becket asked, "What's wrong, Bess?"

"It's that nuisance Forest. He has been pestering me again. He just wouldn't leave me alone and would have followed me up here if the captain of the guard hadn't barred his way."

"Is he still outside?"

"I don't think so. I heard him warning the captain that he would fetch his master."

Becket asked Bess to follow him into the bedroom where Richard sat at his brother's bedside. He pulled Bess's discarded clothes out from under the bed and threw them at Richard.

"Put these on!" Becket ordered.

Richard held the dress up against him said, "Becket. This isn't going to work. Even the most foolish of soldiers isn't going to mistake me for a servant girl, even wearing these rags."

"Don't worry," Becket replied. "When I have finished, you'll be able to fool the soldiers below and at the main gate."

Calling Bess over to him, he pulled out his penknife.

"Bess, I hate to do this but I'm afraid it's necessary, and you do want to help Richard don't you?"

Bess nodded as he took out the scissors from the handle of the knife and began to cut her long auburn hair. She pulled away, but Becket looked into her confused eyes and she seemed reassured. The floor was soon covered. When he had finished, she shyly pulled her headscarf over his handy work and looked away shyly.

Becket called to Richard, "Bring the hooded cloak over here," and then to Bess, "Please gather up the hair."

Becket pulled a candle from its holder and began to drip the hot wax onto the ends of Bess's strands of hair. Pressing them firmly onto the edge of the hood of the cloak, he added more wax. He repeated the process until the seam of the hood was completely covered in Bess's unmistakable auburn hair and then placed it on the table to allow it to set. Richard started to laugh.

Becket pulled Bess to one side and put his hands gently onto her shoulders. "Bess, when the soldiers realise that Richard has managed to escape, you're bound to be suspected. The soldiers need to think that you were ordered by the princes to cut your hair. So, I'm afraid that you're going to have to spend the night locked up in the castle. I'm sure your father will be worried, but I don't know how else to protect you."

"It's all right, I understand, but do you really think this will work?" replied Bess.

"Well, the soldiers all seem to recognise you by your distinctive hair. So, I think that they are unlikely to question Richard as long as he keeps his head down and ignores their jokes and whistles."

She nodded and Becket looked around the room for something to tie her hands. He couldn't find anything suitable, but noticed a trunk sitting at the base of the bed. He opened it, threw in a bed sheet, and using the corkscrew on his penknife made some air holes at each end. He gestured for her to step inside.

"We don't want you suffocating do we?"

Bess carefully stepped inside and when she had signalled she was comfortable. Becket gave her a playful punch on the arm.

"Thanks Bess. We wouldn't have had a chance without your help. After we have given Richard enough time to reach the boat, I will ask Will to get the soldiers to rescue you."

"Don't worry, Becket. I will be fine. It will do my useless brother good to prepare supper. I have slept in far worse places than this."

Becket let down the lid and beckoned for Richard to help him lift the cannonballs and place them on top of the trunk.

"I will send Will on an errand," he explained to Richard. "The less he knows the better for all of us. I will go and find him and see if he can try and get a note through to Brackenbury. Hurry and put on Bess's clothes and say your goodbyes to your brother."

Becket found Will as usual sitting by the window below and handed him the hastily scribbled note. Returning to the apartments, he found Richard dressed in Bess's clothes. Becket looked him up and down grimly.

"Try putting the hood up. Maybe that will help."

Richard did as he was told. Becket grinned.

"The red hair really does the trick. Stoop a little and keep your head down, I'm not sure even her father would be able to tell the difference."

"Nervous?" asked Becket.

"A little, but very excited. It's going to work, Becket."

"Fingers crossed, in an hour or so you will be safely aboard ship and heading overseas."

"Thank you Becket. Without you…"

"Just don't get caught. Bess needs rescuing from that trunk sooner rather than later and don't worry about your brother - he will be fine."

Richard shook his hand and after taking one last look at Edward, left the room and headed downstairs.

Becket gazed at the older boy sleeping peacefully and whispered to Bess, "Are you all right in there? He's just left. We shouldn't have to wait too long."

"I will be fine, but what about you?"

Becket hadn't considered his own plight. The Duke was bound to point the finger at him. He would need to find a place to hide and work out how he was going to get back to York.

Becket sat on the floor with his back against the trunk and rifled through his satchel once again. He was edgy. The plan had to work. But what if something horrible happened to Richard? It would be all his fault. Chatting with Bess to pass the time, he came across the chocolate bar he had bought at Swinford Stores. It all seemed so very long ago. The chocolate tasted wonderful and he poked a small piece through one of the air holes in the trunk.

"What is this Becket?" he heard Bess ask.

"Try it. It's called chocolate. I'm sure you will like it."

"*Mmmmmm*. I've never tasted anything like it in my life. It's so, so sweet and melts on the tongue! Do you have any more?"

Becket looked guiltily down at the empty wrapper. He had devoured the bar in record time. There was a commotion below and the sound of footsteps on the staircase.

He jumped up and bolted to the door just in time, as it trembled under a fearful pounding from the soldiers.

"Open the door in the name of the King!"

He was trapped. Richard must have been discovered. What was he going to do? The loud thumping continued followed by the sound of the door being forced again. The rusty bolt held for a few seconds, but eventually flew across the room and an irate soldier burst in with a crash.

"You are under arrest in the name of the King."

Becket fished inside his satchel and pulled out the fizzy drink and groped in his pocket for his penknife. Shaking the can, he punctured it in several places with the corkscrew. The fizzy liquid exploded out of the holes and sprayed into the soldier's face and eyes, temporarily blinding him. Seizing his chance, Becket sprinted past and out of doorway. Almost stumbling in his haste, he heard the soldier shouting after him.

"Stop him! Don't let him escape, but beware he has magic."

The soldiers below backed away as Becket leaped the last few stairs and made for the door. Shaking the can vigorously, Becket sprayed the remaining contents at the guards and disappeared out into the garden.

Becket kept to the shadows, ducking under the portcullis and down to Traitors' Gate. The bleak, rushing water of the river looked forbidding and Becket knew that it would mean certain death to try and swim his way to safety. The frantic shouts and heavy running footsteps of the soldiers seemed to surround him.

He needed to find a safe place to hide and hope the note had found Brackenbury.

The hungry lions were making a hell of a racket. Of course, the menagerie! That might work. Nobody would think to look for him in the zoo - most of the soldiers were petrified of the curious beasts.

He took a chance and dashed down an unguarded stairwell below the main gate. Reaching the bottom, he peered warily into a gloomy semi-circular chamber. Along the circumference of the room there were about a dozen cages dimly lit by burning torches. The place appeared to be empty. Sweat was pouring down his face and he stopped to wipe his face, when he heard a low growling coming from the corner of the room. Becket tensed, ready to run for the stairs. There it was again – a low grumbling. Then he spotted a greasy, flabby man, lying on a dirty straw mattress and snoring loudly.

Beside the man was a bunch of keys. This had to be the animals' keeper. Becket squinted into the dark cages; a trio of emaciated lions paced up and down, and two bony leopards growled at him, baring their sharp white teeth. In the next cage was a black bear chained to the wall and in the furthest cage was full of tiny jabbering, monkeys making the most awful din. Becket studied the mad monkeys. They didn't look so fierce and their crazy antics were actually quite entertaining. Becket picked up the set of keys as the keeper spluttered and muttered something before farting and rolling over. There was a basket of fruit and vegetables in the corner, Becket grabbed as much as his pockets would carry. Creeping back to the monkey's cage, he began to cautiously try the keys in the rusty lock. None of them seemed to fit. Finally, one turned easily and the cage door clanked open. Returning the keys, he went back to the cage and stepped inside. The monkey's raced over, whooping louder and louder, but the keeper slept on. Becket threw them some fruit and looked around.

In the furthest corner of the cage there was a straw-filled den. It looked like a dog's kennel or an over-sized rabbit's hutch. Becket squeezed inside. It was a good hiding place. As he lay on the rank straw, he wondered what had happened to Richard and hoped Bess had been released from the trunk. What was he going to do? Whatever he tried it just seemed to get worse. He had tried his best for the princes, but now he needed to look after himself. Somehow he would creep out in the morning, escape the castle and find a way to York. He would track down Brackenbury. He would have to help him – he had promised. Becket was totally exhausted. Was this bad dream never going to end? He rubbed his forehead, trying to massage the pain away.

"Please help me! Tell me what I need to do. I want to go home. I can't stand this much longer," he urged the pendant.

Perhaps, that was the point. The pendant itself wasn't magic – it couldn't tell him what to do, it just led the way. It was all down to him. For some reason, as his aunt had chosen him, the pendant had chosen his family. He must be here for a reason. It wasn't by pure chance. He felt bewildered and laying his heavy head down on the scratchy straw, too tired to think any further, closed his eyes and tried to shut out the lions' roars and the snores of the keeper.

CHAPTER 10

THE EVIL PLOT

Light streamed into the cage from above. Becket heard the muffled footsteps of the keeper. He had finally awoken from his stupor and was muttering to himself as he shuffled around the chamber. Becket heard the sound of a heavy metal door being dragged open. At the back of each cage was a small set of steps leading to a grate in the ceiling that led to the viewing gallery above. The lions roared with impatience as they waited their turn and Becket realised that it would only be a matter of time before the monkeys were also turned out for the day. He needed to get moving and although he could easily dodge the keeper, he had no idea how he was he going to get past the soldiers above. Becket slipped out of the cage. The bear lay on its belly looking wretched. Becket gazed at the savage looking manacle and chain fastened around its hind leg; suddenly wishing he could set the poor animal free. He crept over and picked up the keys then rushed to the bear's cage, filling his pockets with fruit on the way. Opening the door, he stepped inside, rolling some apples toward the bear. The beast was nonplussed and lay motionless with its forlorn eyes staring back at him. Becket edged toward the manacle - the keys jangling in his hands. He couldn't believe he was doing this - one swipe from the sharp claws would be the end of him. Inching closer, he managed to place the smallest key into the lock of the manacle. It turned instantly and the shackle dropped to floor with a clank. Becket ran out of the cage as the bear, realising that it was free, stood up on its hind legs, stretched and let out a deafening roar. Becket moved over to the monkeys and opened their cage. They raced out and were soon cavorting around the room. The bear plodded out suspiciously, sniffing the air as it made its way to the bottom of the staircase. The monkeys were screeching, tearing the mattress to pieces and the din soon brought the keeper wobbling down the stairs. Having reached the bottom, he stopped - his eyes widened as he spotted the bear standing on its hind legs and roaring angrily.

The man scampered back up the staircase, followed by the monkey, whooping and shrieking. The bear followed, as did Becket, keeping a safe distance behind. At the top of the stairs, Becket stopped and marvelled at the pandemonium outside. The monkeys were up on the ramparts and were tugging at the soldiers' tunics and hose. One of them had managed to steal a beret and was wearing it with a comical jaunty tilt. The soldiers looked on bewildered at the havoc. Then the bear came waddling out of the stairwell. The bear let out a roar, hell-bent on inflicting its revenge. As some of the soldiers hopelessly tried to keep it at bay with their wooden pikes, Becket was able to dart out of the stairway and legged it toward the exit.

Becket skidded to a halt. But what about the princes? How could he abandon them? They were helpless without him. But what could he do? History had already been written. How could he change the past and even if he could it may have catastrophic consequences? It was time to think of himself, nobody else would help him. Becket turned to go, but his legs wouldn't move. He knew deep down that the pendant wanted him to rescue the boys. He had to go back - he needed to save the princes in order to save himself! That had to be it. Reluctantly, he turned, and cursing himself, crept back past the soldiers onto the main concourse.

The air was full of screaming guards and the growling bear as Becket made his way back toward the Garden Tower. A monkey wearing a beret scuttled past him holding a wine bottle on its way toward the kitchens. Becket smile soon faded. The entrance to the apartments was packed with soldiers – the Duke had clearly doubled the guard. Instinctively, he jogged toward the White Tower, bounding up the wooden staircase. His would try and make contact with the princes when they came to the chapel for prayer. The vast, high-ceilinged main chamber of the tower was deserted, but there was nowhere obvious to hide. The sound of footsteps on the stairway gave him little choice – he rushed towards a shiny suit of armour and started to jam himself into it. He had just placed the visored helmet over his head when two men walked into the room. It was so hot inside the suit and he couldn't see much through the narrow visor, but he could hear the unmistakeable haughty tones of the Duke and another voice that sounded like Bray. Becket stood perfectly still; fearing he may topple over and began to listen to the hushed conversation.

"Well Bray," said the Duke. "Luckily my man, Forest, foiled the escape attempt of the youngest royal brat. Their mother is obviously behind it, perhaps with the helping hand of that annoying little spy who seems to be everywhere."

"Yes, Your Grace," Becket heard Bray reply. "Have your men captured the little nuisance? My mistress is most keen to retrieve a valuable pendant that he has stolen from her."

"Unfortunately not. He is proving most elusive."

"That's most tiresome. I have a score to settle with that popinjay."

"Indeed, as we all have," sighed the Duke.

"Back to business," said Bray, "You are aware my mistress is most anxious for you to deal with the princes as soon as possible?"

"That's all very well," answered the Duke, "but Brackenbury has directed that they are not to be relocated."

"Why so? I thought he was away with the King in York."

"He is, but a rider arrived yesterday carrying a note ordering that the blasted Doctor Argentine be admitted to examine Edward."

"And?" asked Bray

"The darned fool has ordered that the prince is not to be moved until his health improves."

"Is it not possible for Your Grace to overrule Brackenbury?"

"Unfortunately not. He has the King's ear, and being the Constable of the Tower, he holds authority here. I'm a little confused as to how he came to hear of my plans."

"Are your physician's treatments not having…the desired effect on Prince Edward, Your Grace?"

"Strangely not. The doctor doesn't understand it. He tells me he would have expected some results by now."

"Well I'm sure Your Grace doesn't need reminding that we won't have a better opportunity, with the King in the North along with Brackenbury."

"I'm well aware of that. It's all very well for Lady Beaufort to be issuing orders from the safety of her house at Lathom and with Morton living comfortably at my expense in my castle at Brecon; it's been left to me to resolve this unpleasant business. If the boys cannot be moved, I'm not sure what to do."

"I have been told that the brothers pray daily in the small chapel. Is that correct?"

Becket couldn't believe what he was hearing. The two evil men were openly planning ways of disposing of Edward and Richard.

"Are you suggesting we do away with the boys in the holy chapel? Heavens, it's a place of worship and protected by God, man!" shouted the Duke.

"Shush! Please lower your voice, Your Grace. I am not suggesting anything. But I am sure that your man, Forest, must know some men, discreet fellows who for a few coins would forget the sanctity of the church long enough to…"

There was a silent pause, but then he heard the Duke continue.

"I don't like it. I don't like it one bit. After this unpleasant matter is concluded, somebody will have to inform the King and I'm guessing that's likely to be me. After all, these boys are his nephews! His own flesh and blood!"

Becket heard Bray tut impatiently, but then continue coolly, "Your Grace, I thought Bishop Morton had explained to you that you will be doing the King a great service. He will be most grateful to you."

"That's as maybe, but this is a most unsavoury business."

"It is indeed, Your Grace, but on its completion the pathway to the throne for my mistress's son, Henry Tudor, will be clear; and as agreed, the lands that you covet will be yours. And you will have a senior place in Henry's council as promised."

There was another silence. Becket wondered if they had left the room. He had to get out of the stifling armour. He was flagging.

"It will be done. Take word to your mistress that I will be at Brecon within the week and report there to the good bishop," said the Duke.

The room was silent. Becket waited a few minutes until the heat of the armour was finally too much and pulled off the helmet. The coolness of the room hit him as he sat down and removed the rest of the suit.

He wiped his face on the arm of the hoodie. He had to find the chapel. An open doorway at the far end of the chamber seemed as good a place as any to start. It led to a staircase winding down into the depths of the castle. Becket cautiously started down, but almost immediately began to feel giddy, so stopping to steady himself, he looked down as his pendant which once again had started to pulse and was throwing out a purple light illuminating the dark stairway. The blasted thing had suddenly come to life again and was growing hotter and hotter. Was it trying to warn him? If only he could figure out the key to its powers - it held the answer to everything. He stumbled on, the air thick with damp, the steps slippery with water. Becket stopped. In front of him, blocking his path was a pile of rubble – there was no way through. He would have to go back. The pendant was going crazy. It's purple light beaming in the half-light. Becket felt short of breath, his head swimming, as the pendant beat even more madly. He stumbled back up the stairs, falling into the corridor above; he rested his head on the wall, breathing heavily. The pendant once more becalmed. It seemed to be teasing him.

Becket looked around him and spotted a door fastened with a large iron bolt. He jiggled with the bolt and stepping through, found himself in the chapel. This had to be where the princes took their daily prayers. At least he had solved that problem. The room was deserted and the narrow stained-glass windows cast long multi-coloured shadows over the wooden pews. Becket walked toward the altar searching for a place to hide. The pews were the obvious choice – not perfect, but would have to do. As he lay there, he thought back to the conversation between Bray and the Duke. It now all made perfect sense. He was witnessing history - the two small skeletons, the pile of rubble. This was not a scene from a film where the hero lived happily ever after – this was all too real. He knew he had to try to get the princes away. Somehow their safety was inextricably linked to his own. If he could get back inside their apartments – it would buy him time to come up with a plan.

The unnerving silence was disturbed by the sound of footsteps followed by the repetitive chanting of a priest. Peering over the pew, he spied a clergyman standing at the altar - and sitting in front of him, on their knees with their hands clasped in prayer, were the princes. The prayers went on and on as Becket tried to think of a plan. Perhaps the priest would leave them alone to pray. The rhythmic chanting finally came to an end and as the priest motioned for the boys to rise they followed him back down the aisle. Damn!

He would have to take a chance. Becket hissed at Richard as he dawdled past, "Psst! Psst! Richard, it's me, Becket."

Richard hadn't heard him.

"Richard! Over here. It's me!"

Richard looked down with a start.

"Sshhh!" Becket put his finger to his lips.

"Father, if you do not mind, I should like to remain a little longer for some further private prayer," said Richard.

The priest smiled and replied, "Of course, my son. I will inform the soldiers. They can come back for you in a short while. I fear your brother is unwell and needs to rest. I will return shortly."

The priest led the Edward from the room. As soon as they were gone, Richard rushed up to Becket.

"How did you get here? I was sure you had been captured and were locked in the dungeons."

"It's a long story," Becket replied. "But you need to find a way to get me back into your rooms."

"Why? Are you mad! The Duke has doubled the guard and there are now so many soldiers that I don't know how we are going to find a way to smuggle you in or to get us out."

The priest would be back soon. Richard looked around the room.

"I've got it!" he shouted, running up the aisle and dragging Becket behind him. He opened a large empty wooden trunk that was sitting at the back of the room and gestured for Becket to jump inside. Becket looked at Richard dubiously, but he had no ideas of his own. Richard grabbed a white linen cloth from a nearby table, threw it at him and rushed out of the room. This wasn't going to work! Becket sat up in the trunk feeling ridiculous as Richard returned carrying two small cannonballs and placed them inside the trunk beside him. Repeating the trip several times, the trunk was soon full of the heavy iron balls.

"I'm sure the soldiers won't bother checking inside and even if they do, as long as you remain perfectly still underneath the cloth they may not notice you."

Richard shut the lid, and after waiting for a few minutes Becket heard his muffled voice explaining to the guards.

"The trunk is full of cannonballs. Sir Robert said I could take as many as I wanted. I need you carry them to my state rooms immediately."

Becket waited for the guards' reaction. He prayed they wouldn't look inside. Luckily, after a brief pause, Becket felt the trunk being lifted, followed by grunts and groans from the soldiers as he was transported slowly out of the chapel. The journey seemed to last forever and on a couple of occasions, much to his horror, the trunk was lowered to the ground. It was just the soldiers taking a break and when he was finally set down, he heard Richard's muted voice saying,

"Thank you, that will be all. You can leave us now."

After a moment the lid was opened, the cloth removed, and Becket blinked in the light. He got out and stretched.

"Well, I'm surprised that worked."

As Becket helped Richard pile up the cannonballs beside the window, he noticed Will staring at him, ashen faced. The unfortunate boy kept continually crossing himself and mumbling.

Becket winked at him.

Will said, "I thought you had had it... I really did! I thought you were off to Tyburn and that was the end of you! The Duke was furious and was screaming at the soldiers to find you. I thought you were bound for the noose for sure with no one to pull your leg."

"So did I, Will," replied Becket. "But thankfully I'm alive and well and still in one piece. How's Bess?"

"She is all right. The soldiers found her in the chest and everyone seemed to believe her story."

"Thank God!" exclaimed Becket. "Do you think you could fetch her? Time is short, but I think I may have another plan and hopefully this time it will work."

As Will loped from the room, Richard looked at Becket curiously. "Another plan? What is it Becket? How are we going to dodge all the guards?"

"I'm afraid it will have to keep until I speak to Bess. Now tell me what happened. What went wrong? You said you nearly escaped."

Richard said that he had passed through the guardroom below without any problems. The disguise deceived the soldiers and he had joined the crowd as they queued to leave the castle. Everything seemed to be going smoothly until he reached the final gateway. Forest called out Bess's name. Richard had ignored him, but Forest had persisted and grabbing him roughly around the waist, the hood of the cloak had fallen and Richard was discovered. He was marched straight back to the apartments and the Duke was all for moving them to the White Tower immediately. Fortunately, Brackenbury's rider arrived in the nick of time and they were given a reprieve.

Becket twisted his hair.

The door opened and Bess bustled in.

"Thank the heavens you are safe, Becket!" she cried, rushing over and hugging him.

They both hastily took a step back and stood apart red-faced.

"Bess, I'm fine, but I'm afraid I need to ask for your help again. This will be the last time, I promise," said Becket.

"Well, I'm just pleased to see you alive. I'm happy to help as long as you don't cut off any more of my hair!" joked Bess.

"Do you think you could find a way to deliver a note to Lady Woodville at Westminster?"

Bess thought for a minute and then responded, "Yes I'm sure I could. My father will forbid me from making the journey, but I am sure he will find a way to help us."

"Good," replied Becket and turning to Richard said, "Will you write and sign a note if I dictate it to you?"

Richard nodded, sat himself at the table and wrote the following note as Becket hastily dictated:

Dearest Mother,

Please arrange for a boat to be anchored as close to the Tower as is possible tomorrow evening. Three intermittent shining lights will signal that we are on our way. Tell them to be ready to set sail immediately. Please do not fail us.
Your ever-loving sons,
Edward and Richard.

Bess took the folded note and said her brief goodbyes. "Becket, please be careful. If you are discovered there will be no escape this time. The Duke is livid and means to see you swing. I will return tomorrow, hopefully with her reply." She then pulled her headscarf tightly over her butchered locks and left.

Becket followed Richard into the bedroom. Edward's groans were louder than ever. The elder brother lay on the bed clutching his badly jaw. His speech was slurred and his wild eyes looked up from the bed.

"Becket, I am very pleased to see you, but where is Doctor Argentine? I need something to relieve this pain."

"I am afraid he has been sent away by the Duke yet again, although thankfully he left instructions that the poisonous drafts should cease immediately," replied Richard.

Edward howled. "I do not think I shall be able to stand this pain much longer."

Richard helped his brother sit up and drink a little wine. "This will help you sleep, dear brother, but it's all we have I'm afraid."

Richard and Becket left Edward and went back into the next room and sat at the window overlooking the garden. Richard grinned, noticing Becket's carved initials on the wall. Becket offered him the knife and Richard started to carve his own initials. Suddenly, Becket snatched back the knife and started scraping at the stone at the base of the iron that barred the window. It crumbled easily, and he had soon made a large indentation in the wall. He tried pulling on one of the heavy bars and it budged slightly.

Richard looked bemused as Becket whispered, "Where's Will?"

"He's sitting on the window ledge down below watching the boats on the river."

"Can you call him, please?" asked Becket still digging furiously at the stone.

Will entered and stood awkwardly chewing at his dirty, long fingernails as Becket called him over to the window.

"Will, I have a task for you," he said.

Will groaned and fidgeted. He stared down at his shabby shoes.

"Don't worry, you won't get into any trouble I promise," reassured Richard.

The tall boy watched fascinated as Becket scraped away at the stone around the base of the bars at the window. Will seemed intrigued by the knife.

"Do you like the knife, Will?" asked Becket.

"It's magical. I have never seen the like of it before."

"Well if you scrape away the stone until the bars become loose, I will make a present of it to you, but if anybody enters the room you must stop immediately and make sure nobody sees what you have been doing. Is that a deal?"

Will pulled at his black, greasy hair, "I won't get into any trouble? And the knife will be mine?"

Becket nodded and handed him the penknife. Will took it carefully as if it were made of glass and began to scratch at the stone, pursing his lips in concentration.

Richard and Becket went back to the bedroom.

"It's all very well removing the bars from the window, Becket, but we would be certain to break our necks if we jumped from that height."

"I know. I have a plan. I just need a little more time to work on the finer details."

They heard the voice of the Duke of Buckingham booming out orders to the guards below. Richard hastily lifted the curtains that surrounded the four-poster bed. Becket crawled into the narrow space and lay on his back as the Duke marched into the room.

"Good day, Your Highness. I trust you are feeling better," he heard the Duke say.

Edward groaned and the Duke continued, "It has been brought to my attention that you have both requested a private audience with a priest here in your apartments."

"My brother is too ill to continue the journey to the chapel," answered Richard firmly.

"That's as maybe, but I feel it is most important that you take prayer in God's anointed church and I am sure your uncle, the King, would concur. I propose a compromise. I will agree to your request as long as you both attend the chapel at Vespers each day."

"But I told you that my brother is too unwell to move," countered Richard.

"Then I'm afraid he will have to do without religious instruction."

Becket lay perfectly still under the bed. The Duke was scheming to get the two boys into the tower. He couldn't let it happen – it would be the end of them. Looking idly at the mattress above him,

Becket noticed that in the place of the wooden struts that supported modern mattresses, there were a series of interwoven ropes pulled tight and knotted. He recalled a tour of a castle he had taken with his parents, where the guide had explained to them that the origin of the popular saying *Sleep tight; don't let the bed bugs bite!* Referred to the tightness of the ropes that supported medieval beds and the heavy curtains that surrounded them. The idea being if the ropes weren't tight enough, the person sleeping above would fall through the bed and that the curtains once drawn, would keep the insects at bay.

"So are we in agreement? If you are at Vespers tomorrow I will permit you access to a priest. If not, you will have to do without," said the Duke and left.

After a few minutes, Richard's face appeared and he helped Becket out from under the bed.

"I don't like the sound of that. He's up to something," said Becket, brushing himself down. "He is determined to get you into the chapel. You need to be away from here before tomorrow evening. I hope Bess brings us good news."

As Richard prepared to retire for the night, Becket asked him, "Can you swim, Richard?"

"A little," he replied curiously. "My father used to swim in the ponds at the palace in Eltham. We used to stay there during the long hot summers to avoid the plague. I am not a strong swimmer, but I could probably manage to swim...the length of this room."

Becket nodded, but said no more. After a little while Richard gave up waiting for an explanation and went to bed.

Will fell asleep at the window. Becket opened his satchel and fingered the rather useless lollipop sticks. He switched the torch on and off, and discarding the packet of caustic soda and a couple of old plastic water bottles, dug down deeper into the bag. Some old party-poppers, the mouldy whizz-bangs and an unopened packet of chalk sticks. What a rubbish assortment. How he wished there was something more useful that would help magic him and the princes away. If only the wretched pendant would finally do something useful and spirit them to safety. That was too much to hope for – or was it? Nothing seemed real any more.

Jittery, his mind couldn't settle; sleep was impossible. Bess just had to get the message to Lady Woodville. Without a waiting boat, any attempt at escaping would be futile. Will, still holding the knife in his hand, was snoring and chuntering. Becket picked at his dirty fingernails - it was going to be a long night.

After breakfast, Becket and Richard examined Will's handi-work. He had done a great job - the bars came away easily. Becket peered out into the dark morning and down into the garden. The cold air bit into his face and made his eyes water. It was a long way down - too far to jump. Richard had been right. To the left of the window, but just out of arm's reach was the large tree where he had fired the arrow. It was impossible to reach even the closest of its branches. But maybe… Becket's eyes brightened. The tree might be the means of an escape after all!

The sound of hooting soldiers below signalled the arrival of Bess. Becket was nervous. He knew everything depended on her success. She ran into the room in tears and collapsed into his arms sobbing.

"What's wrong, Bess? What's happened?"

Bess couldn't answer. Tears streamed down her face. He noticed a crumpled piece of paper in her hand.

"Bess are you all right? Sit down and tell us what has happened."

Bess sat down and handed over the note.

It confirmed that the ship would be there as requested. Thank God! At least the plan could now go ahead. Tenderly lifting Bess's hands from her face, he passed her a napkin.

She blew her nose loudly and started to slowly explain.

"It was horrible. It was so awful. I think he may be dead!"

She started to cry again as he tried to calm her.

"Bess, slow down. Who's dead? Tell us exactly what has happened."

"My father took the note to Westminster. He gave it to the priest and waited all night for a reply. He arrived home at daybreak with Lady Woodville's answer," sniffled Bess.

"Well that's great news. Why all the fuss and tears?" asked Becket putting his hand on her shoulder.

"When I reached the castle… It was so dreadful," sobbed Bess.

He passed her another napkin and waited impatiently for her to continue.

"It was Forest. He kept calling out to me. I tried to ignore him, but he wouldn't give up. He grabbed me and pulled me down a dark staircase. I tried to fight him off, but he was too strong. He kept trying to kiss me and I must have lost my temper - I shoved him as hard as I could and he stumbled and fell back against a cage. It was unlocked and the next thing I knew, a lion pounced on him. I heard him scream. I couldn't help him - I just ran straight here. Oh my sainted God! I'm sure he is dead. It was so horrible. It was all my fault"

"Did anyone see you?" asked Becket.

Bess shook her head.

"Good."

Richard came over and said, "Thank you, Bess. That rogue had it coming to him. Be assured, you will always have my family's appreciation and gratitude. I will make sure nothing happens to you. You have my word."

Bess coloured and after blowing her nose loudly, left for the kitchen.

"Bess, we are going to need your help again. Is it possible you could come back at the evening bell?" asked Becket as she walked to the door.

"Another one last time, I presume?" Bess answered with a tired smile. "Of course I will come if I am able."

"I promise, this will definitely be the last time. Because if this plan doesn't work, there won't be another chance!" Becket added grimly under his breath.

When she left, Becket beckoned for Richard to follow him into the bedchamber. He approached Edward and gestured for Richard to help him.

"I am afraid I need to move you over to the chair."

Edward's was soon sitting comfortably in a chair nearby.

Becket dragged the straw mattress from the bed and started to untie the knotted rope that lay beneath. With Richard's help they soon had it uncoiled and were left with a thick length of rope.

"We are going to use this to escape through the window?" asked Richard.

Becket coiled the rope into a neat pile.

"The problem is, Becket, the guardroom lies directly below the window and they are bound to spot us."

"I have a plan. Come and sit by your brother and I will explain."

The three boys huddled together as Becket explained.

CHAPTER 11

THE BOY WIZARD

The two princes sat at either end of the long table as Will and Becket served them their evening meal. The mood was subdued and neither seemed very hungry.

Edward laughed as three colourfully dressed musicians entered the room, "I thought they might lighten the funereal mood a little," he snuffled. "It feels like the Last Supper and if this is truly the last time I see your ugly face, younger brother, then I would rather my last memory be of your pathetic dancing than a face filled with sadness."

"There's nothing wrong with my dancing. Our sisters saw to that – I spent hour after hour partnering them."

Edward raised an eyebrow. "Whatever you say, dear brother."

He looked very ill with his swollen jaw and deathly pale face. He looked at the end of his tether. His sweat-soaked hair was plastered to his head and his dull eyes teased Richard once more.

"Your dancing has about as much grace as a herd of wild boar charging through a muddy field."

The minstrels started playing their instruments - a small harp, a wooden flute and a cymbal tapped rhythmically by the third. The music was pleasant and Richard entertained them with a peculiar sidestepping dance. The young prince stepped to the right then to the left before making a low sweeping bow. These actions were repeated again and again and Becket thought Richard was very accomplished. Edward had closed his eyes and his head had slumped onto his chest. Ensuring he was comfortable, Becket ambled over to the window and sat next to Will. Black Will seemed to be mesmerised by the calming melodies. He had finally finished scraping the stone at the window and had begun to whittle away at a piece of wood. Becket poked the boy in the ribs playfully as they both marvelled at Richard's dancing. The door suddenly opened and a flushed Bess entered the room. She skipped toward the two boys, but was accosted half way across the room by Richard, who begged her to join him. Bess reluctantly agreed and hand-in-hand they continued the peculiar dance.

Bess was an even better dancer than Richard, and Becket wondered how she found time to learn such a complicated routine. All girls knew instinctively how to dance, Becket decided, although the memories of his mother's gyrating antics at family parties still made him cringe. Richard, noticing Becket's admiration, gestured for him to take his place. Becket coloured and looked horrified - he had always hated dancing, but was left little choice as Bess grabbed him by the hand and dragged him into the middle of the room. Richard nodded his encouragement as Becket attempted to mimic the dance steps. He felt ridiculous, but Bess's constant promptings left him little choice. More than once he stumbled as he bowed too low. He wasn't having much fun, but Bess held his hand tightly and refused to let him escape. Will clapped his hands and laughed so loudly at his misfortune that he almost fell out of the window, and Richard parodied his stumbling steps so perfectly that even Bess had to stop, as she was crying with laughter. Their fun was interrupted by the booming dong of the evening bell.

Becket knew the moment had arrived to put his plan into action. After the musicians had been dismissed, Richard shook his elder brother awake.

"Is it time little brother?" Edward murmured.

"Yes, I'm ready for my great adventure."

Edward clasped his brother's hand and sitting himself up with a struggle said, "I wish you God speed. Be careful, but my brother, remember you are the son of a king and descended from the noble family of York. You have a lion's blood coursing through your veins, but do not forget your promise. To be king may be our family's birthright, but is also riddled with danger, anguish and misery. Take the opportunity to build a tranquil life away from all this treachery. A life where you can love and trust the people close to you. I wish you luck and happiness my bold little brother."

Edward coughed and laid his head back on the chair. Richard stroked his brother's matted hair gently and re-joined the others.

"Will, we need your help. Are you strong enough to raise the portcullis below? The winch is very heavy, but we only need it to be raised a little so that Richard can crawl underneath," said Becket slowly and deliberately.

"I will get into such... trouble," he stammered. "And the soldiers won't let me anywhere near it."

"Don't worry about the soldiers. Bess will distract them with the remains of the supper. They are so greedy that they won't be able to resist the leftovers and once they are in the guardroom," Becket held aloft a cloth pouch, "hopefully these little devils will do the rest."

"What's in the bag?" asked Bess.

"Black henbane seeds. I have collected as many as I could from the basket the doctor left behind. I need you to drop them into the fire as you leave and it's really important that you close the door behind you, so they can work their magic. I just pray that the doctor wasn't exaggerating when he told us of the weird effect that they can have on the mind and body. It's a bit of a risk, but I have no better ideas."

"Will, I want you to take this note to Sir John Grene as soon as your job is done. I promise that you won't be implicated," explained Becket.

Will looked doubtful. But Becket took the penknife out of his pocket and continued, "I promised you this knife, and as soon as you have raised the gate it will be yours."

Bess took Will by the hand and whispered, "It's important, Will. Please will you do this as a special favour for me?"

The combination of Bess's pleading and the lure of owning the knife finally persuaded Will to agree. He nodded and Becket thumped him on the back.

Becket turned to Bess. He beckoned her to join him at the table where he emptied the contents of his satchel onto the table. She marvelled at the contents: the multi-coloured balloons, the whizz-bangs, and was even fascinated by the clear plastic bottles. Becket blew up and knotted a balloon and grinned as she watched in admiration when he gently patted it toward the ceiling. He shone the torch at the tapestries on the wall, illuminating their gaudy colours.

"Please make this evil sorcery go away Becket. I don't like the light without fire. Please!" moaned Bess cowering.

He switched off the torch, and picked up a packet of balloons.

"I need to show you what I want you to do with these balloons. It's really important. But it's very simple as long as you can throw. I'm sure you'll be fine."

Becket brought over a basin and two large jugs of water. Filling the balloons with water and carefully tying the ends in knots, he placed them into the bowl. After watching for a few minutes, Bess began to help and they had soon filled about a dozen balloons with water.

"The yeoman who guards the gateway to the river seems a bit of a coward. I'm sure he'd run at the slightest sign of danger, so if we can create a distraction, it would make it easier for Richard to slip into the river and swim to the waiting ship."

Becket weighed one of the balloons in his hand.

"Back at home, we call these water bombs..."

And throwing one of the water-filled balloons at the stone wall, he laughed at their reaction as it exploded with a loud splat, water splashing all over the floor.

Bess covered her ears and Will winced at the loud thwack as he repeated his actions.

"They make a great noise and a hell of a mess when thrown with enough force," Becket explained, beginning to enjoy himself.

He then asked Bess to try, which she did with great success, but he had to restrain Richard from repeating her feat, explaining that they needed as many of the balloons as possible. It was essential that they surprised the jumpy yeoman and kept him occupied long enough for Richard to sneak past.

"Position yourself at the window, next to the portcullis, and as soon as Will has raised the gate, let fly with these at the guard. Understand?" he asked Bess.

"Do you think it will work?" she answered.

"I'm not sure, but from Will's reaction just now, it has to be worth a try. Bring over the remaining vinegar please."

Becket filled one the clear plastic bottles halfway with the caustic soda he had bought for his aunt, and the other with a similar amount of vinegar. Bess and Richard looked baffled.

"Don't worry, it's a trick I learned at school. I just hope it works."

Becket explained his plan for the final time.

"So, Richard will climb out of the window, sneak under the portcullis and swim out into the river after signalling three times with the torch. Will, you raise the gate, and Bess will distract the guards with the food and then attack the yeoman with the water bombs."

"But what about the soldiers below? They aren't fools! What if after finishing the food they decide to return to their posts?" asked a doubtful looking Bess

"Leave them to me," Becket answered with a tremor in his voice, "Hopefully the henbane will do the trick and give you the time you need."

Becket walked over to the window and removed the bars from the crumbling stone. He looked out into the cool, dark evening - the dim light from the guardroom illuminating the causeway below.

Richard looked over his shoulder and said, "Becket, even if I manage to drop down on the rope, the soldiers are bound to see me and that will be the end of the that. That's if I don't break my neck in the process."

Becket ignored the young boy and gestured for Will to help him carry the chest over to the window. He placed all the cannonballs inside, barring the smallest one. Picking up the rope and tying one end firmly around the trunk, he knotted the other end securely around the small cannonball. He carried the ball to the window and looked out into the night. Richard joined him and stared vacantly in the direction of his focused gaze.

Becket pointed to the tree in the garden to the left of the window and explained, "If I can manage to throw the ball through the gap in the trunk where the large branches part, it should be heavy enough to act as a counter-weight and either wrap itself around one of the branches or at the very least drop to the ground on the other side. Then hopefully the rope will be taut enough to help you to climb down into the tree. Once you make it there, it should be easy for you to drop down onto the garden wall and then down to the gate without being seen."

Richard looked at the rope and the tree. "But Becket, how am I going to climb in these useless things?" said the boy looking at his soft leather shoes.

Becket scratched his chin. He realised Richard was right. The shoes weren't made for climbing and it was possible that he might slip and fall. Looking down at his own feet, he began to remove his beloved trainers.

"Try these on! You look roughly the same size."

Richard pulled the trainers on easily, as in reality they were a little too large. "Heavens!! These are wondrous. I have never worn anything so comfortable. It feels like the floor is cushioned with feathers."

Becket sorrowfully eyed his trainers and slipped Richard's shoes over his dirty, white socks.

"Take off your cap and cloak," he ordered. "You won't be able to climb or swim in those."

He then handed Richard two uninflated balloons.

"When you reach the river, blow these up and place them under your shirt. They may help keep you afloat while you wait to be rescued. Here's the torch. It's easy to use: just press that button there to turn it on. Remember you need to signal three times. Is there anything else?"

Richard shook his head. "Thank you, Becket. Without you I don't know what we would have done."

"Don't thank me just yet. I could be sending you to a watery grave," replied Becket.

"It's going to work. I'm determined for the sake of Edward and my family that I get away from here. This could be our last chance. I hold my family's future in my hands and I'm determined to succeed. I just have to. But Becket, what's going to happen to you?"

Becket knew he had to escape, but first his plan had to work. He just prayed that somehow his pendant would rescue him from this nightmare. He longed to be back home, away from scheming dukes, murderous old ladies and conniving priests, but for now he had to show no fear. His newfound friends would need all their courage to pull off his madcap scheme.

"Don't worry about me," he heard himself reply. "I will be fine and anyway somebody has to look out for Edward. Now is everyone ready?"

Becket weighed the cannonball in his hand. It was smaller and heavier than a basketball, but he was sure that he could shoot it through the narrow gap in the tree. He recalled watching a programme about gauchos in Argentina and marvelling at their skill with a throwing weapon called a "bola". They were similar to the cowboys in the old West and charged about on horses throwing a rope weapon that had weights attached to the ends. They would swing them violently above their heads and throw them with incredible accuracy at wild animals. The heaviness of the weights entangled the poor beast's legs, bringing them crashing to the ground. He hoped that the same concept would work with the cannonball and the tree.

He looked at the tree. It was no more than three metres from the window. He could do this. It was just the same as shooting baskets. Closing his eyes, he tried to imagine he was on a basketball court and taking one last look at the tree to judge the distance; he swallowed hard and flung the cannonball. The heavy ball arced through the air toward the tree. It began to dip; it was going to fall short! But then, almost as if powered by Becket's hopes, it seemed to glide before hitting the tree with a thud, teetering momentarily, before agonisingly rolling down behind the trunk and wedging itself between the branches. The chest was dragged toward the window with a screech, but held firm, and miraculously the rope tightened just as he had envisaged. It had worked! He could hardly believe it! Rushing to the chest and quickly testing the rope, re-tightening the knots, he was satisfied it was fit for purpose. He just hoped it would hold Richard's weight long enough for him to reach the tree.

The first part of his plan had worked.

He turned to Bess. "Are you ready to take the food? Do you have the bag of seeds?" Bess nodded.

"As soon as Richard climbs outside, go downstairs and give the food to the guards. Shut the door behind you and come back up and collect the water bombs. I'll wait a few minutes for the seeds to work their magic and then go down and do my best to distract the guards whilst you raise the gate and bombard the yeoman."

Becket's accomplices nodded. He turned to Richard.

"Good luck. Remember, don't jump down from the tree until you see the gate raised."

Richard held his hand out to Becket.

He shook it and said, "Come on, there's no time to waste."

Richard scrambled onto the window ledge and tentatively lowered himself down onto the rope. Grasping the rope between his hands and feet and gripping it tightly with his legs, the young boy shuffled slowly along. Although the rope bowed, it held firm. Richard slipped, but managed to right himself as his feet scrabbled against the wall of the tower. Thank goodness he was wearing the trainers - without them he would have fallen. Richard inched along the rope toward the safety of the branches of the tree. Just a metre more.

Becket had just begun to congratulate himself when he heard the bellowing Duke of Buckingham below.

"Quick, Bess. Hide under the bed! Will, help me replace these bars and sit down there on the trunk in front of the window. Hopefully he won't notice the rope."

He heard footsteps on the stairs and hastily threw on Richard's hat and cloak and had just jumped into a chair by the fireplace when the door burst open and in walked the Duke followed closely by a squat, ferret of a man. Becket pulled the cloak tightly around him and pulled the beret down over his eyes. He stared into the fire, away from the Duke's gaze. Edward, having been disturbed by the sudden entrance, looked confused, but thankfully noticing Becket at the fireplace in his brother's discarded clothes, regained his composure and said,

"We are resting. Why have we been disturbed?"

"I have come to make sure that you are going to keep your side of our agreement and that you will be attending prayers in the chapel."

"I told you that we would and I intend to keep to my word," Edward replied.

Becket was scared. He hoped that the Duke wouldn't speak to him.

The Duke paced around the room, picking up an apple from the table.

"This is my man, Persivall. He's come down from Brecon having been in France on the King's business. He's aiding me as that idle fool Forest has disappeared, no doubt holed up in some bawdy tavern, getting blind drunk as usual."

Becket heard Bess gasp.

"What was that?" asked the Duke.

"Just me groaning. The pain in my jaw and teeth grows worse by the day. I am certain that I won't be an encumbrance to you and my uncle for much longer," said Edward.

Becket looked at Will. Thankfully he was perfectly placed between the Duke and the window. The weasly little man peered in Will's direction, but the rope and the trunk went unnoticed. The Duke munched his way through the apple and asked Edward again to make sure they attended evening prayers, then swanned out of the room without a backward glance.

As soon as the door slammed shut, Becket dashed over to the window.

"Great!" Richard had almost made it to the tree.

Bess clambered out from under the bed. Becket handed her the bag of seeds.

"There's no time to waste! Richard will be spotted if we don't hurry."

Bess picked up the tray of leftovers, straightened her dress and left the room.

Becket rummaged in his satchel and pulled out the packet of chalks. Hastily daubing them onto his face, he was soon covered in white chalk. He then painted a blue circle around each eye and drew ragged red lines across his forehead.

"God's truth! You look like a demon or evil spirit that has risen from the dead!" exclaimed Edward.

Becket pulled Richard's dark cloak closer around his shoulders and after giving Edward a departing thumbs up, picked up the two water bottles, took one last deep breath and strode out of the room. His legs trembled as he walked down the stairway. Drama had never been his strongest subject, but he knew that this would have to be the performance of his life if his plan were to succeed. He pulled out the party-poppers and striding into the guardroom, fired the noisy toys into the crowd of guards.

The heat of the room was overwhelming and the choking fumes clawed at the back of his throat, causing him to cough. Thank God! Bess had done well - the seeds were having the desired effect. Becket swayed in the heat and smoke and putting a linen cloth over his nose and mouth, he ploughed on into the room. The haze stung his eyes; they started to water, blurring his vision. Two of the soldiers lay on their backs writhing in front of the fire, another was sitting cross-legged in the middle of the floor hugging himself whilst the remaining were stumbling laps of the room, flapping their arms like a flock of demented birds. The guards didn't seem to notice Becket and before they could make any sense of what was happening, he began to chant loudly in the deepest voice that he could muster,

"I AM THE GHOST OF THOMAS A BECKET. I HAVE BEEN RESURRECTED TO SEEK REVENGE ON THE KING'S SOLDIERS. I COME TO PROTECT THE INNOCENT AND SEND THOSE THAT DO NOT SEEK REDEMPTION TO HELLFIRE AND DAMNATION."

Hastily blowing up the rocket balloons, Becket let fly. They whizzed wildly around the room, screeching and causing panic. The seeds had worked way better than Becket could have imagined, but his childish tricks would be useless if their effects were to wear off. He could hear Will struggling manfully at the giant winch as his shaking hands poured the vinegar into the bottle containing the caustic soda. Tightening the lid, he shook it vigorously and removing the linen cloth from his mouth boomed in a sepulchral voice,

"SAINT BECKET HAS COME TO TAKE YOUR SOULS! REPENT BEFORE IT IS TOO LATE."

Becket threw the bottle into the room, where it exploded impressively,

BANG! WHIZZ!

It flew across the room like a crashing spaceship, leaving a trail of spurting white foam in its wake.

"Wowser!"

He had never seen the trick work so well. One of the soldiers started to scream.

"Jesu save me. I repent! I repent!"

WHEEEZ! screeched another balloon, narrowly missing a ducking soldier.

Becket threw some of the whizz-bangs into the fire.

CRACK! BANG! POP!

The men covered their ears in alarm and retreated to hide under a wooden table. Another of the guards took a flying leap towards the wall as if making a final attempt at take-off, but only succeeded in hitting the stone wall...*THUD*...knocking himself senseless.

Becket was almost beginning to enjoy himself, but after inflating some more balloons edged slowly back towards the doorway. He ran out of the room, slamming the door behind him and joined the labouring Will at the giant winch. Quickly grabbing one of the wooden spokes that drove the mechanism, he pulled as hard as he could. Will was wide-eyed and dripping in sweat, but the gate hadn't budged. Becket's added strength seemed to do the trick, as with a screech, the heavy iron gate began to budge. Little by little, centimetre-by-centimetre, it was finally lifting. It had to be high enough for Richard to crawl underneath! Becket left Will to hold the winch steady and joined Bess at the window. The girl was having the time of her life, throwing water bombs at the poor scared guard who could be heard screeching, "The sky is falling on my head! Lord, please save me!"

Picking up the remaining balloons, Becket joined in the fun. Balloons rained down on the guard until he fled screaming for help.

In the moonlight, Becket could just make out the small figure of Richard at the bottom step of the gate. Knotting the last balloon, he pushed them under his tunic and signalled with the small torch before noiselessly entering the dark water of the river. Becket could just make out the outline of the young prince as he battled the strong current, swimming away from the castle until he could see him no longer. Becket turned away. The muffled noises of the soldiers behind the door had stopped. How much longer would they remain in the guardroom? He didn't wait to find out. Grabbing Bess by the hand, he shouted for Will to scarper and darted back to the staircase. Bess rushed up the stairs and he reached into his satchel and emptied all the bubble liquid onto the floor before bounding up the staircase into the apartments above. Wildly wiping the chalk from his face and shouting at Bess to hide under the bed, Becket ran over to the window and peered into the night outside. Happily, there was no sign of any guards giving chase and he hastily untied the rope, throwing it down into the darkness of the garden. There was a loud hubbub below, soldiers howling in pain - they had found the bubble liquid.

Once again putting on Richard's discarded clothes, he huddled up to the fire. Before long, two soldiers burst through the door, looking wildly about the room, seemingly searching for the strange boy wizard.

"What has taken you so long? By the sounds of the ruckus downstairs, you have been drinking! You call yourself guards? My uncle, the King will hear of your negligence," shouted Edward.

The two bewildered and dishevelled soldiers bowed respectfully.

"We are sorry Your Highness, but we thought we saw a mysterious boy-sorcerer running up here," said one of the soldiers.

"Of course you did you buffoon. He could have killed us. He ran into the room, removed the bars from the window as if they were made of straw and flew out into the night like a giant raven."

Becket almost burst out laughing, but just pulled the cloak higher over his face and feigned sleep as before.

The soldiers stood bemused in the middle of room until Edward dismissed them with an irate regal wave.

Bess emerged from under the bed, and Becket removed the cloak and sat down on a chair beside the bed and let out an exhausted sigh.

"All those childhood stories about Merlin had some use after all," said Edward with a weak cough.

The young prince looked very ill. His pale face and sunken eyes made Becket fear the worst.

"Did Richard make it?" he wheezed.

"I'm sure he did," replied Becket, trying not to think about the fierce current of the river.

Bess walked across the room, and after dipping a napkin in some water, dabbed it on Edward's burning cheeks.

"That was great fun, if a little frightening, but what's the plan now?" questioned Bess.

"Well, if Richard isn't present at prayers then the Duke will know something is wrong and order an immediate search. Then we will both be found."

Becket puffed out his cheeks. He felt empty. He needed some sleep. He didn't want to have to think any more. He was sick and tired of formulating plans. It was almost as if his brain was shutting down in self-defence. He just wanted to curl up in a ball next to the fire and forget everything.

Edward coughed. "It must be almost time for Vespers. The soldiers will be coming for me soon."

Becket toyed with Richard's beret. The heavy satin material didn't seem suitable attire for the summer, but then neither did the long cloak.

"There's only one thing we can do," Becket murmured. "I will have to go with you in Richard's place."

"You go to prayers, Becket?" cried Bess. "They will lock you up as soon as they see you."

"Not if I wear his cloak and hat. It's obvious we look very alike and I've already fooled them twice before. There's no reason it shouldn't work again, as long as I keep my head down and my face covered."

Bess looked imploringly at him. "It's too much of a risk, Becket. If they catch you this time…"

Bess stifled a sob with her apron. Becket didn't dare think of the consequences - the memory of severed heads still fresh in his mind.

"Well I'm guessing nobody has any better suggestions and at worst, it will buy Richard a little more time and enable you to sneak back to the safety of the kitchens."

Bess looked distraught and busied herself making Edward as comfortable as possible. "Becket, how are you going to get out of this place? I won't let you take any more risks… "

Becket looked at Bess. He had no idea. He knew she was right. He jiggled with the pendant, stroking the smooth surface of the dark stone between his fingers. It held the answer, but would it come to his rescue? Why had it had sent him on this fantastic journey? If he completed his mission, would it send him home? Avoiding Bess's tear-swollen eyes, he stared into the depths of the fire. The nightmare was close to the end- one way or another!

CHAPTER 12

LADY SWINFORD

Becket looked up as Will entered the room. The awkward boy sat by the window and started to whittle at a small piece of wood with his newly acquired penknife. "What are you whittling, Will?" he enquired.

"A boat. I like boats," Will replied.

"Have you seen any boats tonight?" asked Becket.

"Boats don't sail at night. Even if they did I wouldn't be able to see them." He stopped whittling and poked at a hole in his shoe. "'Cept tonight. I did see a boat. I would have missed it, but there was this flashing light, like fireflies, only it seemed it was there one minute, then gone the next. Kept seeing 'em. Then I noticed it. A little hoy with its sails raised, silently heading down river."

Flashing lights and a boat heading out to sea. Was it Richard signaling with the torch? He must have made it! Becket had liked Richard the first day that he had met him. It was almost as if he had known him before, somebody from his past. With his help the young prince had escaped, away from the fearsome Tower of London.

It was almost time for him to join Edward on his trip to the chapel, and as he looked around the chamber he had a feeling that it may be the last time he would see the apartments. He was certain that the Duke wouldn't let Edward return; it was only a matter of time before he was discovered. He winced as he recalled the shocking conversation between the Duke and the treacherous Bray. Something terrible was going to happen.

Walking over to Bess, he forced a smile and teased, "Getting used to the short hair? Maybe you will set a trend."

She pushed her locks further under her headscarf. "Becket, what's going to happen to you?"

"I shall be all right, Bess. I'm sure I will find a way - Brackenbury should have received my note by now and will be riding back to the rescue." Becket looked down at his feet awkwardly. Bess didn't reply. They knew this was goodbye. Becket would miss her. He had never felt this way about anyone before.

Four soldiers entered the room. Becket hid his face inside the hood of Richard's cloak as they helped Edward to his feet then took his place beside him as the soldiers hustled them out of the room. Will was still sitting at the window whittling away at the wood. Bess, with tears forming in her eyes mouthed silently,

"Stay safe. I shan't forget you."

The White Tower loomed in front of them. Becket looked around hopefully. In his heart he knew there would be no escape this time, he would have to trust fate and pray the pendant would do the rest. If only Brackenbury was here. What was taking him so long?

The night was chilly and Becket shivered as they trudged up the wooden staircase and into the tower. Edward was struggling, frequently stopping to catch his breath, much to the frustration of the captain of the guard. They were led into the chapel, and after helping Edward down the aisle the soldiers left them alone. The flickering shadows cast from the candles licked at the floor adding a spooky aura to the deserted chapel. Becket felt uneasy – where was the priest? Edward's breathing was shallow, the short walk had left him bathed in sweat. He fell to his knees before a large, gold cross and, holding some beads, starting mouthing some private prayers. Becket knew this was his chance to make a run for it, but how could he leave Edward? He had promised Richard he would look after him. If only Brackenbury would arrive. Two men entered the room carrying a large wooden trunk, placing it at the back of the chapel. They were filthy and didn't look like soldiers. What were they doing in the chapel? Becket mimicked Edward and bowed his head, pretending to pray as he waited for the men to leave, but they just stood at the back and watched.

There was still no sign of the priest and Edward had closed his eyes and began to sway. Becket put out his arm to steady him and was astonished to find that the sick boy was frozen and clammy. He needed a doctor. Becket would have to risk capture - Edward wouldn't last much longer. He ran down the aisle to call for help, but the two men barred his way. Becket backed away, but the men followed. One of them held a sack in his hands. This couldn't be happening. There was no other way out. Edward had collapsed on the floor. Then, the men were upon them - their rancid breath and reeking bodies made him gag. Becket was wrestled to the floor, strong arms pinning him to the stone floor.

The second man stared down at Edward, "This one's done our job for us by the look of him."

Becket wriggled and writhed, pushing at the man's stubbled face, trying to free himself, but he was too strong; his calloused fingers grasped Becket's throat. Where was Brackenbury? He had sworn to help – he had promised. Becket couldn't breathe. Suddenly the man screamed out in pain. The pendant had once again sprung to life and was throbbing, its stone burning, but the mans grip tightened. Becket was blacking out - his head spinning. It wasn't fair. He didn't want to die. It didn't seem real, almost as if he was watching himself in a horror film. But then - the foul-smelling sack was over his face and even as Becket realised that he had lost his final battle, he began to fall into a spiraling, sinking darkness, choking with fear, until nothing.

Becket opened his eyes and stroked his throat. It was so sore: his skin felt itchy and scratchy. He put his head between his legs and took some deep breaths. At last the room stopped spinning. Then he felt a prod. He looked up into the face of the grey haired man. Behind him was the eerie Quire Screen. He was back in York Minster.

"Are you all right, Becket?" the old man asked. "You don't look all that good." The old man was dressed as before in his pristine black suit and was wearing his ridiculous bowler hat.

Becket felt the bile rise in his throat and again put his head into his hands, swallowing hard and looking down at the floor.

"You look like you have been in the wars young fellow. Sit still a little longer, although I fear the Minster will be shortly closing for the day."

Becket looked around the cathedral. A gaggle of tourists were dawdling toward the exit as some bored guides stood chatting. He felt for the pendant dangling on his chest and clasped his shaking leg. It wouldn't stop - he thought back to the coarse sackcloth and his fight for breath. The pendant had rescued him, as somehow he always knew it would.

"You need some fresh air. Let's pop up the tower. It will do you good. You will soon feel better," said the old man twirling his walking stick.

Talk? Becket just wanted to go home. Who was this man anyway? The last thing he felt like doing was hauling himself up to the top of the tower, but nevertheless, he soon found himself toiling up the spiral staircase.

The old man glided upward. Becket legs were leaden, each narrow step an effort. At last, he stepped out onto the roof into the cool summer breeze. The old man looked out over the parapet and down at the city below.

"Marvellous isn't it, Becket? The wonder of York. Such a rich history. Truly the capital of the north."

He was home. What a relief just to see cars on the road. He thought about his mum's smiling face and soft hands and choked back a sob. The shock had finally wrenched the grief from him and as he tried to stem the tears, oblivious, the old man continued, "Think of all the people through history who have walked those streets below. The Roman legions garrisoned here, the legendary highwayman Dick Turpin, who rode the length of the country from London to York on his trusty Black Bess to escape justice. Did you know Guy Fawkes was born in York? And that a famous Royalist and Roundhead battle had taken place during the English Civil War, there by ruins of the old abbey? And of course, the most famous son of York, the King of the North, Richard III himself made his grand entrance during his royal progress in 1483."

Becket's eyes narrowed. The mention of Richard and the progress made him think of Brackenbury and his pride at joining his king.

"The streets were lined with scarlet cloth in his honour. There were feasts and pageants, the likes of which had never been seen before. He invested his young son as Prince of Wales at this very Minster. They say Richard loved his wife and son very much and was devastated when they died within a year of each other. His son was only your age."

"Richard III has such a tarnished reputation, but you know Becket, he was the last King of England to be killed in battle and died bravely fighting his enemies at Bosworth Field."

Becket listened attentively.

"When he made that last desperate cavalry charge, were the death of his wife and child on his mind? Did he feel he had anything to live for? Maybe he had other regrets, weighing heavily on his soul. It's always been assumed that he was responsible for the deaths of his two nephews, the Princes in the Tower. Perhaps the fates of those boys, in addition to the death of his family, were at the forefront of his thoughts on that fateful summer's morning as he made that last dash through the morning mist toward his enemy, Henry Tudor. Either way the outcome was the same. The Stanley brothers turned their coats and joined battle on the side of Tudor, changing the course of English history forever. Richard was slain as he fought his way toward Henry and the rest, as they say, is history. And you know Becket, the royal line remains unbroken from that day right up to our present Queen."

So Lady Beaufort had achieved her goal! Her son had won the battle and had become king. She had spawned a dynasty that had lasted centuries. Becket looked at the excited old man. Why he was telling him all this?

"You're looking better. The grogginess will soon pass and you will feel as good as new."

Becket nodded. His sore throat had oddly disappeared.

"You know, Becket, most of the answers you seek are within you."

"I don't…understand."

"You are so young, but you are the future. That pendant you wear around your neck, I'm guessing you have many questions?"

Becket looked down. What did this funny old man know about his pendant?

The old man stared at him intently.

"It was found in the depths of York castle many years ago. A relic from the Templar knights," continued the old man. "The key to its energies is a mystery. It is written that the knights had special powers, holy powers from God, to defend Jerusalem. So many myths and mysteries."

Becket didn't understand. The Templar knights? Then he remembered the book.

"Your aunt is a brave and determined lady. I'm sure she will explain when she feels the time is right. It is not my place to burden

146

you, but take care; others may seek the pendant's powers. They mean to protect their dynasty at all costs. They know the power of the Abraxus stone and fear it above all else. I have already said too much, but remember, Becket, I will always be here if you need me. I can do no more."

The old man's eyes misted.

"Becket, do not too look to hard for the truth. Sometimes it is looking you straight in the face."

Becket studied the old man closely. As he clutched his bowler hat in the wind, Becket noticed a tiny tattoo on the inside of his wrist. It was faded, but looked like two knights riding on a solitary horse. Becket remembered the creepy crypt at Westminster. Was it the same image? What did it mean? The old man pulled down his immaculate white cuff and once more the tattoo was hidden.

"Always try and make a difference. Learning to give yourself selflessly is the secret, young fellow. Listen to your aunt. You may not be able change history, but you can always try to give fate a helping hand."

Becket twirled his long blond hair. Who was this cryptic old man?

"Tell me about the Templar stone. It's some kind of time machine right? And the Quire Screen its portal. But I don't understand. Why me? Why was I sent? How did my aunt get the stone?" Becket urged.

"So many questions. In time you will know all. It's important you speak to your aunt. She knows much, but I do not know how much she would have you know."

"How do you know my aunt? Who are you? I need to know. I'm the one who almost...died!" Becket choked.

Before he could ask any more questions, the old man straightened his hat and floated off down the staircase. Becket rushed after him, stumbling down the stairway and finally reaching the bottom, looked around the cathedral. The old man had vanished.

Becket yawned loudly. He was so tired. Taking a seat in front of the Quire Screen, he looked up at the weird kings. This is where it had all begun. The extra statue was no longer there. He wasn't surprised. Once again there were only fifteen statues. A tap on his shoulder startled him.

"Hello, young man. You look a tad lost. Can I help at all?" asked a smartly dressed guide.

"I'm looking for my friend," answered Becket. "He just came down from the tower, but I seemed to have lost him."

"Really?" replied the guide. "I didn't see anyone. In fact, I have just been rounding up the strays as we are closing for the day and thought the place was empty until you appeared."

"But you must have seen him," answered a bewildered Becket. "Grey haired old man wearing a bowler hat and carrying a walking stick."

The guide looked at Becket sympathetically and replied, "Well I'm sure I would have remembered him, but maybe he slipped past me. He's probably outside, and I'm afraid I'm going to have to ask you to leave as well."

Becket made his way through the gift shop and out into the fresh evening air of the square. There was no sign of the old man. His Chopper bike was still standing at the railings where he had left it. Becket slung his satchel over his shoulder. The same little old lady was sitting on the bench. She was wrestling with a particularly crumbly meringue, but managed a sweet smile in between mouthfuls. He thought it odd. Perhaps the old lady sat there scoffing every day? Either way, she must get through a lot of cake.

It was time to go home - back to his aunt's house. Jumping onto his bike, he sped off through the busy town, past the closing shops and crowded pubs, dodging the tourists and out of York.

What was his aunt going to say? She would have alerted the police. How was he going to explain where he'd been? It all seemed so fantastic. He pedalled hard, desperate to get home – back to the warm reassurance of his aunt's house. The Chopper sped along and he soon left the urban district of York and was once again riding through the countryside as the yolky-yellow sun began to dip. The road was deserted and Becket began to enjoy the clean air and tranquility until he heard the guttural sound of a vehicle chugging along behind him. He daren't look behind; the last thing he needed was another run-in with the bully from the manor. With a grinding of gears, a small white van accelerated passed him; causing his bike to wobble and he skidded to a stop. Becket was annoyed. That had to be the same van - the one that had run him off the road. At least it hadn't stopped.

However, as Becket rounded the next corner he bit his lip. The van was parked at the side of the road. Maybe if he got enough speed up, he could dash past. Then the doors of the van swung open and two men jumped out. One started to shout at him, but was cut short by a second, shorter man, who ordered him back into the van. Becket and the second man stood motionless, staring at each other, like two gunfighters in a Wild West film, until at last, the man said with a nasal twang.

"Sorry about that, young fellow. I didn't see you in the fading light. Can I offer you a lift?"

The man pulled the bike toward him and started wheeling it towards the van. "My name is Parker. I'm the chief steward at Swinford Manor."

"But... I'm fine..." Becket argued.

"If you don't mind squeezing in the back with your bike, I'll give you a lift home. You have just moved into the gatehouse haven't you?" asked the man ignoring Becket's protestations.

"The bike's OK. I can ride..."

"Nonsense. Jump in."

Becket eyed the back of the van. It was madness to get inside -it went against everything he had been taught by his parents. Trying to think of an excuse, he backed away, but he was helped inside along with his bike. The door slamming behind him. The van accelerated away. He tried the door, but it was locked.

There was no air and the powerful smell of petrol made him feel ill, but at last the van ground to a halt. He could hear the two men's muffled voices, followed by some footsteps crunching on the driveway. The door swung open and Parker helped him out. Becket was horrified. They were parked in front of the manor.

"Don't worry, young fellow," Parker reassured him. "I thought the least I could do was offer you a hot drink and a chance to tidy yourself up a bit. I'll take a look over your bike, after all it was my rash driving that almost caused you to crash."

They both knew that the bike didn't need fixing. Parker led him into the dimly lit hallway. It smelled soggy and the air was stale.

"There's a bathroom to your left where you can freshen up. I will arrange a hot drink and some cake. Just in the sitting room across the hall."

Becket washed his face with warm water. It felt wonderful to wash away the crud and to feel clean again. Crossing the hallway, Becket entered the sitting room. The drab room was dark, heavy curtains were drawn across the window. A small fire fizzled in the hearth, its feeble glow casting eerie shadows across the room. Becket sat down on the edge of a worn leather chair. The dry cake had seen better days, but he was starving and wolfed it down. The sweet hot chocolate scalded his throat, but it tasted incredible - he certainly wasn't missing the small beer. Just as he was feeling more relaxed, the door behind him opened and a familiar looking old lady came into the room, ominously stopping to lock the door behind her. She was wearing a long grey dress and around her shoulders wore a black scarf. Becket was flabbergasted. It wasn't possible. The same heavily lidded piercing black eyes; the same threatening pallid face - Margaret Beaufort stood in front of him.

"Hello young man. My name is Lady Swinford. I am the owner of this house. I hear you had an unfortunate accident whilst riding your bike in the lanes," she said, showing no sign of recognising him. "I hear you have moved into the old gatehouse. The lanes in the wood at night can be very dangerous. I suggest you take more care in the future."

Becket gaped at the old lady.

She looked like Margaret Beaufort. She spoke like her, dressed like her, but it was impossible? She must have died five hundred years ago and yet here she was standing in front of him, living and breathing and not looking a year older than when he had last set eyes on her at Westminster. He leaped from the chair, making for the door, but she clutched his arm firmly and said, "I live here quite alone, young man. I have the need and desire for total privacy. I do not like trespassers especially meddlesome boys. Most of all, I do not like people trifling in my affairs. Be warned! You are young and have much to learn. Stay out of my way or I promise you will live to regret it!"

Her pinching grip stung his arm and he tried to pull away as she continued, "Before I let you run along, I believe you have something precious that belongs to me." She held out a wrinkled palm. "Give it to me now – it will be better for you in the long run."

Becket gulped. It couldn't be Margaret Beaufort? It had to be some sort of modern day relative. But how did she know about the pendant?

She stood glaring at him, tapping her left foot repeatedly on the worn carpet.

"You seem confused. Pass over the stone. You have no idea what you have become involved in."

Becket backed away from her piercing eyes. Then, he noticed, hanging loosely on the front of her gown – a similar pendant! It was the same Star of David shape and size, but instead of a deep purple stone set in its centre there was a blood-red stone, with weird Greek-like writing etched across it.

Lady Swinford reached out a skeletal hand, her bony fingers snaking towards him, "Give me which is mine…"

Her words were lost in a sudden hissing freezing mist, that came from nowhere, enveloping all but her clawing hand as it grabbed at Becket's pendant.

"*Yeeeeooooow*"

A deafening noise screamed around the room.

Becket dropped to his knees, covering his ears – trying to drown out the din. His head was bursting. He had to get out. Then the noise suddenly stopped.

Becket opened his eyes. The room was quiet. The fog had disappeared. The fire still crackled and his hot chocolate sat half-drunk on the side table. Where had she gone? And what was that horrifying mist? He had to get out before she came back and lurching to the door, he found the key in the lock and stumbled out into the hallway.

Becket ran out of the front door, leaped onto his bike and pedalled madly up the gravel drive toward the main gate. Damn! The gate was locked. He wanted to cry. He would have to go back. Slowly circling the house, not daring to look up at the windows, he made his way toward the gate that stood adjacent to his aunt's house. He just prayed it wasn't chained also.

It was impossible. A five-hundred-year-old lady, who would stop at nothing to own the pendant. Well, his aunt could have it back. If she wanted to go gallivanting through time, then that was her lookout. He had had enough. He threw his bike down and strode over to the gate.

It was shackled with a heavy padlock. He would have to climb the wall. He would get his bike later. His feet scrabbled for a hold on the bricks as he tried to grip the stubbly ivy vines, but it was useless. It came away in clumps and he just slid to the ground.

He screamed in frustration. There was no way he could squeeze through the bars. Taking a running leap at the wall his hands tore at the ivy in desperation, but he fell backwards onto the grass. He stood up and kicked out angrily at a bush. Then he saw it. A small wooden arched door, poking out from the torn ivy, no more than a metre high and green with mildew. It looked like it hadn't been opened for years. Becket shut his eyes and pulled at the iron ring handle - the doors opened effortlessly. Without stopping to wonder, he picked up his bike and scurried through.

Cycling through the blackness of the wood he finally saw his aunt's house. A light above the porch flickered, but otherwise the house was dark. Opening the door, he called out to his aunt. There was no reply. He went into the kitchen, and putting his head directly under the cold tap gulped down the clear water as it gushed all over his face. Water had never tasted this good. His stomach gurgled as he nosed in the fridge, stuffing the remains of a pie into his mouth. The sitting room looked the same as the day he had left it. But what had he expected? Throwing himself down on the sofa, he stretched, curling his toes. He was home. Safe at last.

Becket woke to the sound of rain splattering against the window. He could smell vinegar and then a hand began stroking his hair. Opening his eyes, he was startled to see his aunt bending over him. "Becket, thank God you are home. I was so worried. Are you ok?"

He looked up at his aunt's concerned face. She was crying.

"I am such an old fool. I should never have sent you to the Minster ... but I had to know."

His aunt sat down next to him and pulled him toward her.

"How long have I been away?" Becket asked pulling away.

"Only a night and a day," said his aunt.

Becket's journey no longer seemed very real. What was happening to him?

"But the pendant...the Minster.... I went back..."

"Slow down, Becket. You are home now. It's all going to be ok."

Looking down at his feet, Becket saw Richard's shoes! The one's he had swapped for his trainers. At least he wasn't going crazy!

His aunt lifted him by his elbow.

"You should go up to bed. Are you hurt?"

"But aunt I don't understand …"

"Go to bed. We can talk later when you have had some rest."

Becket grew angry.

"But I need some answers. The pendant…I went back …"

"OK. Calm down. Come with me, perhaps we should talk," his aunt interrupted.

She led him through the hallway and into the museum room.

She sat down in an old leather chair and beckoned him to draw up a stool opposite her. She reached out and held his hands. "Did your father ever speak about his childhood?" she asked.

"Not really. He mentioned that all of my grandparents had died before I was born, but that was about it."

"Alfred was never particularly interested in the family," said his aunt. "He always had his head in a book. Well, when I was little girl, not much older than you, our parents died within a couple of months of each other. Your father was sent away to boarding school to finish his A levels and I was sent to live with my Aunt Jemima in a little village to the north of here. She wasn't really an aunt, but she was my mother's oldest friend and kindly offered me a home."

His aunt shifted her gaze to the pendant hanging around Becket's neck.

"Not long after your grandmother died I decided to go through her things. I felt that they would bring me closer to her, almost bring her back to life. Whilst searching through her jewellery box I came across the pendant that you are wearing. She had lots of jewellery - most of the rings on my fingers belonged to her."

So the pendant had belonged to Grandma Bramble! The pendant was a family heirloom.

"Life with Aunt Jemima was very quiet. In truth, a bit dull for a young girl, so when I wasn't attending school I used to visit York and wander around the old town looking in the shops and cafes. I enjoyed my own company and spent day after day alone nosing around the lanes and walking along the old city wall."

"One day I wandered into the Minster, and came across a kindly old man dressed in a black suit."

The old man! He'd said he knew his aunt.

"The old man showed me the Minster," continued his aunt. "Walked me to the top of the tower and told me that the pendant was very special and I was to never take it off. Then, as swiftly as he had appeared he was gone, leaving me in front of the ancient Quire Screen."

"As I have told you before, Becket, all the items in this room belonged to real people who lived real lives. They struggled through difficult times, brought up families and fought for those that they loved. I am so tired, but these things are so very special to me, like old comrades. They remind me of the past, of such adventures; it sometimes feels like I have lived a hundred lives. I'm getting old, with the arthritis and the creaking bones I am no longer strong enough to continue. That's one of the reasons I gave you the pendant."

Becket pulled off the soft leather shoes. They were filthy.

"I regret giving it to you, but you must understand, at that time I was confused, I thought it was for the best. I was so worried it would be lost or stolen and I had to know…whether you also had the power – whether you were the one to continue."

It was incredible. His aunt was also a time-traveller. He had so many questions - about the old man, the Quire Screen, the powers of the pendant and the old lady who lived at the manor house.

"Perhaps I should have waited…you are so young."

"Aunt Lizzie, who lives at the manor house?" Becket interrupted.

His aunt tightened her grip on his hands. "Becket, I have told you before, please stay away from the manor!"

"But…but Aunt, I just…"

"I made a mistake. I have put you in danger. I need time to think what to do for the best."

She got up and walked from the room.

Becket called after her. He deserved an explanation. Why wouldn't she tell him? It wasn't fair.

Becket was tempted to run after her, to demand an explanation. He knew he couldn't sleep. He needed answers. Why was his aunt being so evasive? Looking around the room, he spotted the leather diary sitting on the table. There might be a clue hidden amongst the pages. The fusty book was full of numbers and dates and some lavish writing almost too faded to read. Turning the yellow-brown pages, it suddenly slipped from his grasp and hit the floor with a thud. Oh no! The spine had split and the cover was hanging loosely. His aunt would kill him. Scooping the book up carefully, he placed it back on the table. Maybe she wouldn't notice. It was only an old diary anyway. Then, just as he was about to leave, he noticed a torn set of yellowing papers sticking out from underneath the spine. He pulled it out. It was bound with a black ribbon. It must have been hidden there for years.

Becket untied it and opened out the aged paper, coughing at the dust. It appeared to pages from a diary. He started to read.

The fifth day of January 1492.

On this blustery, inclement day, I supped with a travelling priest. He was passing through the town and needed shelter. I was glad of the company, as it is not often that I have the opportunity to converse with a fellow countryman. After some roasted meat, we sat around the fire and he told some tales of his travels. He had travelled far and wide and seen many things. He recounted a particular story that had moved him much. He stared into the flames of the fire and told me that he needed to unburden his soul as he had somehow relinquished his responsibilities as a man of God. The story he told, awakened in me a pain from the past and perhaps a clue to the mystery that has laid heavy with me these many years.

He was on the northwest coast of France touring ancient churches as he was much taken with their architecture. Seeking lodgings late one night he came upon a secluded house, tucked away in the cliffs above a small bay. The dwelling housed only a lady of middle-years and her young son.

At first she was hostile and would not offer the priest shelter. But on seeing his desperation she finally agreed to give him a bed on the condition that he would under no circumstances converse with her son. She said he was young and his health was very delicate. The priest gratefully accepted, and after a restful night's sleep was readying himself for his onward journey.

As the mother tended the animals, the boy, sought out the priest and asked him about the world and his travels. The boy seemed old for his years and as they talked, the priest asked him about his life. The boy told the priest the most outlandish tale, which at first he put down to a boy's fervent imagination and would have soon forgotten had the mother, on coming across them, not reacted in the most astonishing manner. She turned ashen white, started to tremble and went down on her knees and pleaded with the priest not to tell of the story the boy had told. Under no circumstances was he to reveal their whereabouts. The poor lady was petrified and clearly in dreaded fear of someone. Of course, seeing her distress he readily promised. This was the young boy's story as the priest recounted it to me.

The boy had told him that he was the son of a prince. His father, the bravest man that ever lived, had been locked up in a castle where escape was impossible. But one day a travelling boy wizard, with the help of a beautiful servant girl, helped him fly over the walls of the castle into a mighty river where he swam to a boat that helped him escape to safety across the sea. His father had always taught him that he was also a prince, whose birthright was to be king of this faraway land.

On reaching safety, his father had remembered the loyal servant girl and sent for her. Love blossomed and they eventually married. His father foretold, 'One day an army will seek you out and plead with you to lead them and then you will regain your rightful place as their king.'

The priest had been struck not by the boy's fanciful story, but by the terrified look on the mother's face, which had haunted him ever since. He couldn't banish her from his mind. He said he would never forget her eyes or her long, thick auburn hair.

The diary continued on a second page.

I'm an old now and have had a good life, but can't help thinking of the two young princes so long ago that were once left to my care. I have lived with the guilt that I failed them in their direst hour and yet, this story gives me hope. Did one of the royal princes escape? It seems fantastical, but having witnessed the priest's troubled looks as he recounted the tale, I can't help but want to believe that one of the unfortunate boys managed to escape the Tower and the clutches of those who meant them ill.

Becket winced as he re-read the last lines. Could it be that the boy was Richard's son? Was the protective auburn-haired mother Bess? Did they marry? How could the solution to one of the greatest mysteries have laid hidden in the spine of a book in his aunt's back room? And what had become of the boy? Had the Tudors known that Richard was alive, they would have stopped at nothing to find him. No wonder the boy's mother was so protective and so petrified.

He read on. There had to be more. But it was just a jumble of boring everyday life. He started to roll up the paper but noticed, at the bottom of the last page, so faint that he almost missed it – a signature. He squinted and pulled the paper closer. It said,

John Argentine, Doctor of medicine.

The room seemed colder, the floorboards darker. The doctor - the princes' faithful doctor. It was his was diary. Where had his aunt found the book? She couldn't have known the existence of the scroll as it had obviously been hidden there for centuries. This had to be Richard and Bess's story. Pushing the paper back inside the cover, Becket stretched. He needed a bath and then he would tackle his aunt. He placed Richard's shoes on a chair and left the room.

Becket felt a bit woozy as he walked into the kitchen for break-fast, but the orange juice and bread and homemade jam soon re-vived him. He thought of Bess and her first taste of chocolate. He missed her already. She somehow seemed closer to him than any-one. If only he could see her again.

As he munched on his fourth slice of bread and jam, his aunt asked him,

"Feeling better?"

Her eyes were swollen and red. She looked awful.

"Becket, I owe you an explanation, but you have to realise that this isn't easy for me. The more you know, the greater the danger for you."

Becket stared at her. He felt a sense of foreboding, but also excitement, as he knew he was about to find out all the answers he craved.

"I need a little more time to gather my thoughts, but I will meet you later in York and we can talk. I thought this morning that maybe you would like to visit York public library. They have computers there and I know young people can't live long without the Internet."

Becket hadn't thought much about the Internet, but it wasn't such a bad idea. It was clear his aunt wasn't ready to answer all his questions.

"I suggest you cycle to the library after breakfast. And no trip to York is complete without a visit to Betty's famous tea room, so I will meet you there."

Becket went up to his room. Picking up his inscribed book on the Kings and Queens of England, he turned to the chapter on Richard III. The conventional story - the evil uncle, usurping the throne and doing away with the two young princes stared out at him. It seemed all so matter-of-fact and answered none of his questions. Had he really managed to change the course of history? How could he without altering the course of so many lives? Becket was confused, but even more eager to get to the library. He ran down the stairs and after shouting a hurried goodbye to his aunt, leaped onto the Chopper and started cycling through the wood toward York. He enjoyed the freshness of the day and the clean feel of the wind through his hair as he made good time along the road to York. Having reached the library, he parked his bike and made his way past an austere-looking lady with a pointed hairy chin, and sitting down at the nearest computer, he looked down at his pendant and typed,

THE KNIGHTS TEMPLAR

After the First Crusade recaptured Jerusalem in 1099, many Christians made pilgrimages to the Holy Land. However, though the city of Jerusalem was relatively safe, the rest of the region was wild and dangerous.

Bandits and marauding highwaymen preyed upon pilgrims who were routinely slaughtered, sometimes by the hundreds.

A French knight, Hugues de Payens approached King Baldwin of Jerusalem and proposed creating a monastic order for the

protection of these pilgrims. King Baldwin agreed and granted the knights a headquarters in a wing of the royal palace on the Temple Mount. The Temple had a mystique because it was built upon what was believed to be the ruins of the Temple of Solomon. The Crusaders therefore referred to it as Solomon's Temple, and from this location the new Order took the name of Poor Knights of Christ and the Temple of Solomon, or "Templar" knights.

Becket yawned. He was tired, and losing interest as he scrolled down - then he saw it:

The knights' popularity waned over the years, as they became known to be greedy in their search for land and profit. There were rumours that they had discovered a substantial priceless booty under the old stables of the Mount. It was thought to be Solomon's treasure with plates of gold, precious jewels and even mystical amulets that were said to protect them and make them invincible in battle.

Was his pendant one of the original magical amulets? It seemed implausible, but it was possibly making a little sense at last. Mystical legendary knights with mysterious pendants. Then two hundred years later, charged with heresy, held captive in York castle until their trial at the Minster. Was this the connection? But how had his grandmother come by of one of them?

Now to the princes. What happened to Richard? He typed *"The Princes in the Tower"*. He was once again disappointed to see the usual articles and references to Richard III. There was little mention of the Duke of Buckingham and nothing of Lady Margaret Beaufort. What had actually happened? Had Edward died that day in the chapel? What about Richard? He tapped again at the keyboard, determined to discover the fate of the young boys.

All he found was the standard story,

The two princes were imprisoned in the Tower of London by their uncle, King Richard III and at some point during the summer of 1483 the boys disappeared. The assumption was that they were murdered on the orders of the king, but their bodies were never found.

Becket slammed the mouse down hard on the table in frustration, causing the stern-looking lady to look over at him crossly.

Just then he came across a more interesting article,

Skeletons of two young boys were found two hundred years later in a trunk under some debris at the bottom of disused staircase in The White Tower.

Becket's mouth was dry. The dark, blocked staircase. It made sense, but two skeletons? He remembered Edward limp in the rough man's arms. But he had saved Richard! And why, if poor Edward had died of his illness, would they have concealed his body so carefully in a place where it wouldn't be found? It would have been easier to have a state burial and make it known he was dead. It didn't make sense! It led to the only possible conclusion. The skeletons didn't belong to the two princes at all, but were of two other unfortunate boys whose story would never be told. He read on,

The skeletons were given a royal burial and interned at Westminster Abbey. There have been calls for the bones to be exhumed and tested for DNA, but to this point, permission hasn't been granted by the royal family.

Becket flicked through some more websites. Then he came across another link:

Two pretenders to the throne of England came forward during the reign of Henry Tudor. Lambert Simnel in 1486, who claimed to be

the son of Richard III's brother, the Duke of Clarence. He was subsequently proven to be an impostor, who had been cleverly coached by an ambitious priest to play the part of the royal prince. He confessed and was pardoned by King Henry VII and bizarrely given a job working in the kitchens.

Becket thought of Bess and the roasting hot kitchen and read on hoping to find some mention of Richard.

Perkin Warbeck, in 1495, claimed to be Richard, the younger son of Edward IV.

He read on excitedly. This had to be it! He had finally found the answer.

Perkin was recognised as Richard by his aunt, Margaret of Burgundy, Edward IV's sister, and she funded his invasion of England. After an unsuccessful incursion into Cornwall, Perkin was captured, declared an impostor and hanged as a common criminal at Tyburn on the order of King Henry VII.

Becket prayed the priest story was true. That Richard had kept his promise to his brother and lived out his life peacefully.

Becket was frustrated that the detail on the princes was very repetitive. It shed no further light on the fate of the two boys.

Perhaps nobody would ever find out how the story of the Princes in the Tower had truly ended, but Becket knew that he had more answers than anyone to one of Britain's greatest riddles. Not that anyone would believe him. They would just laugh at a young boy's fantasies. Becket made his way out of the library and back to his bike. His dad would have been amazed at his sudden thirst for knowledge and he hoped his dad was smiling down at him as he cycled, through the streets of York toward Betty's tearooms.

He jumped off his bike and barged his way into the cafe. He was starving. His aunt was sitting at a small corner table, her striking hair tied up in a bun and a thick purple shawl draped around her shoulders.

"Did you find everything you needed, Becket?"

"Yes and no," he answered. "I guess some mysteries will never be solved. Maybe that is the way it is meant to be."

"Very wise, but your father always said that you have been here before."

A large waitress dumped a mound of assorted cakes and sandwiches onto the table in front of them. He tucked in as his aunt nibbled at a salmon sandwich and sipped some herbal tea.

"Aunt, the story you told me about our pendant. Is it a family heirloom?"

His aunt seemed reluctant to talk and carried on picking at her sandwich.

"Did my dad know all about it?"

Aunt Lizzie sighed, "I can't help regretting giving you the pendant. You are so young. I suppose it is only fair that I explain a little more."

Aunt Lizzie tidied her hair, her tired dark eyes looking across the table at Becket.

"As I told you, your father and I were separated after our parents died. We were never close before and certainly not thereafter. I do not think he knew about the pendant. Perhaps, the secret would have died with your grandmother had I not happened upon it and met the old man in the Minster. Maybe things would have been so different"

"But who is the old man? What is his connection to the pendant and our family?" Becket asked.

Aunt Lizzie put her hand to her forehead.

"His name is Beasant. Your Grandmother seldom talked of the past, but often said that our family had once been wealthy. Back in the Victorian times, the family house had been very grand with plenty of surrounding land and many servants. Beasant has offered little over the years, excepting that he once served our family, not quite a servant, but some sort of retainer. It is very sad, but it seems he is locked in time at the Minster, a sort of shepherd, a guardian of the portal – the ancient Quire screen. Something terrible happened to him of which he won't speak, but I know he will always be there to protect us."

"Are you saying he's a ghost?"

Aunt Lizzie winced.

"A ghost? I have learned over the years how easy it is to be lost between times. If that's a ghost, then maybe he is."

"Has the pendant a connection to the Templar Knights?"

Aunt Lizzie perked up.

"Ah, I see you know more than I have given you credit for. I do not know for sure. The pendant draws lines through time. To when and where it sends you, is hard to comprehend, but there always seems to be a reason and it has always made sure I got home safely."

So his aunt had also travelled through time. He was finally getting somewhere.

"The lady at the manor. Who is she? Why does she want the pendant so badly?"

Aunt Lizzie paid the bill and got up to leave.

"Come Becket, we can talk as we walk. This is not the right place to be talking of such things."

They walked out into the fading light of the summer's evening, Becket's aunt leading him firmly by the arm.

"I will tell you some of what I know of the manor and the so-called Lady Swinford, but you must promise me that you will stay away from that place," his aunt said.

"You may wonder why I choose to live in such a spot," she continued. "The truth is I was drawn here by the past."

Aunt Lizzie pulled at her ring on her finger and reluctantly continued.

"Apart from her jewellery and a few old photo albums, your Grandmother left few clues of our family history. One day, leafing through one of her scrapbooks, I found a family photograph titled Christmas 1885. It had taken in front of a manor house. I was intrigued as to its whereabouts, but the photo offered no further clue."

They had reached the old town wall and his aunt started to climb the worn steps. Becket bounded up after her.

"The day after I moved into the Gatehouse, I was investigating the wood and I couldn't resist a peek at the manor. Maybe you can guess what happened next? I couldn't believe it t first. But there was no mistaking it - it was the same house, the one in the photograph. I was a little shocked and have often wondered whether it was fate or whether the pendant had purposely drawn me here?"

Aunt Lizzie had stopped and was leaning on the wall staring into the distance.

"Then I came across Lady Swinford. The less said about her the better, but it seems she has a similar pendant, possibly with parallel powers."

The red pendant with the strange hieroglyphics.

"It seems the stones are drawn to each other, but are unable to meet unless one is relinquished willingly. I think that once together, their power intensifies. She is so determined, but for now remains powerless. I thought by sending it to you… away from here it would be safer. The break-in scared me. I'm sorry Becket, it wasn't fair, but I didn't know what else to do."

Becket felt like he was studying algebra and struggling to follow the teacher. He wished she would be clearer. Aunt Lizzie sat down on a nearby bench.

"But what does she want?" asked Becket.

"I am afraid I do not know for certain and I fear it is likely that the pendant will push you on toward you the truth. Beasant told me to always remember that the historic bloodline of today's monarchy stretches back to the day that the Tudor's took the throne from the last Plantagenet king, Richard III. A dynasty that survives today."

His aunt turned to face him and with shining eyes said, "I often wonder, Becket, if there was a more rightful monarch, perhaps a survivor of an ancient line of kings, a descendant, hiding with their secret, somewhere out there."

Becket thought of Richard. What if the priest had really found Richard and Bess? What if the bones in Westminster Abbey were not of the two boys? Maybe that's why the royal family won't allow DNA testing. That was the point. It was necessary that people thought that King Richard III had killed them. His aunt continued,

"Can you imagine? If the Tudor's were alive today, they would stop at nothing to find the survivor of that line and eradicate them once and for all. You have seen the power of the pendant with its power to transcend time - the ability to travel through the centuries. We appear to be the counter-balance. Our pendant against theirs."

Aunt Lizzie strode toward the bus stop and Becket had trouble keeping up.

"All is not clear to me," she continued, "although God knows, I have tried to fathom the key to the mystery for so many years. You could say it has been my life's work. Why the pendant brought me back to our family home I have no idea. The key must lie inside. But now I am tired, too tired and need some peace."

His aunt sat down on a bench and looked up at him. "Becket, I think it maybe your turn, but I am frightened for you. Please stay away from the manor and if the lure of the Minster is too great, be very careful to never take off your pendant. Whilst you wear it, you will always be protected and I will always be here for you whatever you decide."

Becket was puzzled. It was frustrating. He was so close to understanding, yet his aunt clearly only knew so much.

It was getting dark when they arrived home. Becket felt in limbo. He was beginning to piece together the puzzle, but there were so many missing parts.

After a quick wash, Becket wandered into the kitchen seeking his aunt, but she was nowhere to be found. She surely couldn't have gone out again – it was late. The sitting room door was open and Becket could see a light shining in the museum room at the back of the house. He found his aunt sitting in the leather armchair with a book on her lap. Her hair cascaded over the book, it was so long, grey and thick - it would have been beautiful in her younger days.

She looked up as he entered, hastily wiping her nose on a handkerchief.

"What are you looking at?" he asked.

"Granny's old photograph album. Come and sit beside me and take a look."

Becket pulled up a stool.

The album was falling apart. The photos were all black and white and fading badly. His aunt leafed through the frayed pages. Photograph followed photograph of nondescript black and white images. Austere middle-aged men with pointed beards and stiff high white collared shirts. Large ladies in puffy silk dresses with ludicrous doily bonnets. Children with blank expressions trying to look far older than their years.

She stopped turning the pages and looked at Becket. On the page in front of him was a larger photograph. It was of a group of around twenty, half were children, standing on stone steps in front of a large red brick house. It was Swinford Manor! Only somehow a softer image, the beds full of flowers and the brickwork pristine as if newly built. At the top of the stairs, set apart from the main group, was a collection of servants.

Becket studied the picture. No smiles, a very formal photograph. Then, his eyes lighted upon a young girl to the front right. She was wearing a high-waisted, simple dress, a tumble of thick hair mounded on top of her head like an oversized ball of wool. He couldn't believe it. His belly lurched. It was Bess. The same full lips, wide eyes and freckled face. But how could it be?

His aunt studied him keenly. Becket face burned.

"I see you have recognised the house as our manor," she said, "and by the shocked look on your face you have spotted someone familiar amongst the servants?"

Becket felt breathless. Servants? He looked again at the photograph.

The servant group comprised of a severe looking matron in a somber dress, a younger lady wearing a black gown – the hint of a smile upon her face, an ancient bald man looking every inch the archetypal butler and standing slightly aloof, was Beasant. He was wearing the same formal black suit, bow tie and bowler hat. Becket somehow wasn't surprised.

"Aunt, the young girl ... the one in the front with the thick hair. Who is she? How is she…"

"The one on the bottom right? That's Great Grandmamma Bramble. My mother's Grandmother."

"But it can't be… I know her… I met her… I don't understand."

"That's where I get my long, thick hair," continued his aunt ignoring Becket's confusion. "Apparently it was a beautiful auburn colour, much like my own when I was young. It runs in the Bramble family as does your blonde locks."

Becket didn't know what to say. How could Bess be in a photograph taken five hundred years after she lived? Unless it wasn't Bess? But perhaps a relation. It was too much of a coincidence.

Becket put a hand to his forehead. He was sweating. Was he related to Bess? Was she his ancestor? That was why the pendant had sent him on the journey. If the priest's story was true, if Richard had sent for Bess, then saving Richard had in a bizarre way saved his own family. Saved his very existence. It was too fantastical.

"Becket, are you ok?" Aunt Lizzie looked concerned.

"I'm fine, just a little..."

Becket got up and paced the room.

"Did Grandma never tell you anything of the past? Nothing at all?" he asked.

"Very little, Becket. As I have told you, other than we were once a far wealthier family, she didn't care to talk of our history. You have to remember, I was quite young when she died."

Aunt Lizzie got up and snapped shut the book.

"Come on Becket, you look shattered. Time for some much needed sleep. Off to bed you go. There are no more answers to be found in this old book."

"But...but Bess – we are related? You must know."

His aunt put her arm around his shoulders and led him from the room; Becket almost in a trance followed and stomped up the stairs to his bedroom, collapsing onto his bed.

There had to be a link. To Richard and Bess, the pendant and his family. He reflected on the events of the past week. Was the pendant a family heirloom – a guardian of the past? If so, why didn't his aunt know more? What was he supposed to do? To ensure Lady Beaufort didn't succeed in destroying Richard's remaining family line? Distinguishing the threat to the Tudor dynasty? It didn't make sense. Had he really changed the course of history by saving Richard? How could he have when the consequences of failure would have meant the very end of his own existence? Well he had saved Richard, he was sure of it. Becket pinched himself. He was still here. The same twelve-year old boy who had travelled up from London. It seemed so long ago. The manor held the answer of that he was sure, but for now he would steer clear, until he could find out more. He didn't relish the thought of bumping into Lady Swinford again anytime soon.

Becket shut his eyes – drifting somewhere between consciousness and dreams. He hoped that Bess had found happiness although he felt a little jealous. It was ridiculous, she was probably his great, great... too many greats ancestor. So many questions - his mind clogged full of half-thoughts, with apparitions of Beasant the ghost, the pendant and the Quire Screen and the Templar knights appearing like spectres out of the gloom.

Becket thought about Black Will, of gentle Brackenbury, the tanners with their back-breaking smelly job. He thought of the kind old priest, about Lady Woodville's tears, such adventures, excitement and terror.

Becket rolled over and pulled the duvet up under his chin. It smelled clean. He thought about his parents, how much he missed them, but realised that he no longer had to feel sad. His time in medieval England had given him an inner confidence. It had taught him to look forward and be thankful. Whatever mysteries remained to be solved - he realised having good friends and helping them made him feel good. It gave him a purpose. He stroked the smooth stone of the pendant. It had protected him when he had most needed it and when he was inevitably drawn back to the Minster, he would be ready. He would solve the riddles of the past; he knew he would.

NOTES

Richard III – Richard was killed at the Battle of Bosworth in 1485, two years after having usurped the throne from his nephew, Edward.

Henry VII (Tudor) – Henry was crowned king after defeating Richard in battle at Bosworth. After marrying Lady Woodville's eldest daughter, Elizabeth, Henry spawned the birth of the Tudor dynasty and his son, Henry VIII and children Elizabeth and Mary would all become monarchs of England.

2nd Duke of Buckingham (Henry Stafford) – The once loyal adherent of Richard III changed allegiance and led a rebellion to place Henry Tudor on the throne in 1485. Many people have speculated on his motives. Some suggest that he wanted to claim the throne for himself, others that it was because Richard had denied him the lands that he coveted. There has been a suggestion that Richard had spurned him in disgust when hearing of the disposal of his royal nephews.

The Duke of Buckingham's rebellion failed and he was captured hiding in the disguise of a servant in the New Forest. Despite his pleas for mercy, Richard refused him an audience and had him executed.

Margaret Beaufort – After her son, Henry VII, was crowned King of England, Lady Beaufort became "My Lady the King's Mother" and enjoyed all the riches and privileges that came with the position.

She died in 1509 during the reign of her grandson Henry VIII, having outlived her son by two months.

Bishop John Morton – On Henry Tudor's accession to the throne, he was made Archbishop of Canterbury and given the position of Lord Chancellor of England. In this latter position he managed to replenish the King's coffers through severe and harsh taxation. He became very rich and powerful and died in 1500.

Sir Reginald Bray – Henry VII made Bray a Knight of the Bath at his coronation, and later Knight of the Garter.

He was an able administrator and was given the prestigious and important task of restructuring the King's finances.

He died in 1503.

Lady Elizabeth Woodville – After the marriage of her eldest daughter to Henry VII, Elizabeth became the Queen Dowager. A few years later she retired to a nunnery in Bermondsey where she died in 1492 aged 55 years.

There is speculation that she was forced to leave court as it had been discovered that she had played some part in the rebellion of Lambert Simnel, but perhaps there was a simpler explanation:

there just wasn't enough room at the palace for a "Queen Dowager" and "My Lady the King's Mother".

Cecily Woodville – Was married three times and had many children. She died in 1507 aged 38.

Sir Robert Brackenbury – Died fighting at King Richard III's side at Bosworth.

Sir Anthony Woodville (Earl Rivers) – Brother to Lady Elizabeth and uncle to the royal princes, was executed on Richard III's orders in June 1483, just as this story was about to begin.

Sir James Tyrell – Trusted servant of Richard III. He was in France during the Battle at Bosworth and was subsequently pardoned by Henry VII and appointed the Governor of Calais.

Some twenty years later, Tyrell was arrested on the charge of treason and whilst undergoing torture, supposedly confessed to the murders of the two princes although he was unable to specify the whereabouts of the bodies. He was executed in 1502, although King Henry strangely reversed his attainder five years later.

Doctor Argentine – Was a famous English doctor in the late 15th Century. There is reference to a John Argentine being in attendance on Prince Edward in 1483, but there is some confusion if this was the same man. He became the private physician to Prince Arthur, Henry VII's eldest son, and died in 1507.

Black Will – In Thomas More's famous 'The history of King Richard III' it is mentioned that the princes' familiar servants were denied them and they were left in the keeping of a man called

Black Will or Will Slaughter. Whether he actually existed and what became of him we will never know.

Bess – There is no mention in any of the contemporary accounts of a girl named Bess, but I am sure there were very many hard-working kitchen maids employed in the Tower working at that time.

The Princes, Edward and Richard – Speculation continues about what actually happened to the royal brothers. They were last seen playing in the Constable's garden at the Tower of London in the summer of 1483. Many solutions have been put forward as to their fate and it has spawned a thousand books, but until today's royal family agree to the DNA testing of the two skeletons interned in Westminster Abbey, perhaps the mystery will never be solved.

The White Tower – Is the central tower, the old original keep at the Tower of London. It was built by William the Conqueror in the 11th century and was the tallest building in medieval London.

The Garden Tower – Is now known as the Bloody Tower. Its new infamous name was derived from the assumption that this was the location of the murder of the royal princes. Sir Thomas Overbury was poisoned in the Bloody Tower in 1613 and Sir Walter Raleigh was kept prisoner there for over ten years early in the seventeenth century.

The Menagerie – was first referenced in the 13th century, when King Henry III was given a present of a polar bear.

Subsequently an elephant house and a barbican for lions were commissioned. The latter was situated under the main entrance and became known as the Lion Tower, but is no longer in existence.

In 1816, a sentry on guard reported that he had witnessed an apparition of a bear charging towards him and subsequently died of fright a few days later. Unfortunately, there are no such recorded instances of ghostly monkeys.

The Royal Menagerie was relocated to Regent's Park in the middle of the nineteenth century becoming London Zoo.

Traitors' Gate – Originally the Water Gate until it was given its more infamous name in the middle of the 16th century.

Edward I built it in the 13th century to provide an entrance from the River Thames to St Thomas's Tower.

Knight's Templar seals and pendants/Abraxus stone.
The Templar Seal showing two knights on one horse allegedly symbolized the initial poverty of the order; that they could afford only a single horse for every two men.

Abraxus stones have been found originating as far back as the 2nd Century.

These stones were used as amulets to bring bout power and magic to the bearer.

Abraxus was the name of a powerful deity that they believed top be far superior to the Christian God. Abraxus was a creature that had the head of a rooster, the body of a man and two serpent legs. Many Templar seals have been discovered bearing this strange image. The reason they adopted, like many things associated with the mystical Templar Knights is a matter of speculation.

Printed in Great Britain
by Amazon